HONEYCOMB

Patricia McCowan

ORCA BOOK PUBLISHERS

Library and Archives Canada Cataloguing in Publication

McCowan, Patricia, author
Honeycomb / Patricia McCowan.
(Orca limelights)

Issued in print and electronic formats.
ISBN 978-1-4598-0579-8 (pbk.).--ISBN 978-1-4598-0580-4 (pdf).--
ISBN 978-1-4598-0581-1 (epub)

I. Title. II. Series: Orca limelights
PS8625.C69H65 2014   C813'.6   C2014-901553-4
                     C2014-901554-2

First published in the United States, 2014
Library of Congress Control Number: 2014935397

Summary: Nat loves to sing and hopes her newly formed trio will win a
chance to play at a big music festival, but first she has to learn to trust her
own voice—both on and off stage.

*Orca Book Publishers is dedicated to preserving the environment and has
printed this book on Forest Stewardship Council® certified paper.*

Orca Book Publishers gratefully acknowledges the support for
its publishing programs provided by the following agencies:
the Government of Canada through the Canada Book Fund and the
Canada Council for the Arts, and the Province of British Columbia
through the BC Arts Council and the Book Publishing Tax Credit.

Cover design by Rachel Page
Cover photography by Dreamstime

ORCA BOOK PUBLISHERS
PO Box 5626, STN. B
Victoria, BC Canada
V8R 6S4

ORCA BOOK PUBLISHERS
PO Box 468
Custer, WA USA
98240-0468

www.orcabook.com
Printed and bound in Canada.

17 16 15 14 • 4 3 2 1

For my parents, who always encouraged my love of the arts, no matter what.

One

I don't have butterflies in my stomach; I have big flapping pelicans. I've never been so nervous. In the dark backstage of an old church auditorium, Harper stands in front of me, watching the act that's before ours. She's pulled her dark, curly hair into a pile on top of her head, and excitement sparks off her like a meteor shower. Jess waits beside me, rock-steady as always, her guitar slung toward her back, her hands in her jeans pockets.

The three of us are the last act on the last day of March-break music camp, and I'm hoping the act onstage will never end. Not because five guys doing an all-horns version of "Smoke on the Water" is great. It's weird. But once Brassed-Off is done, we're up.

Why am I so nervous? I've sung in front of tons of people at school choir competitions. But it's easy to blend in with a choir. In three-part harmony, if I suck, I'll stand out. It's the standing out I'm afraid of.

Harper stage-whispers, "We are so gonna bring the house down after these goofs." She glances at me, winces, puts her hands on my cheeks. "Nat. Girlfriend. Breathe."

I take a deep breath.

"Now put your stage face on."

I do my best to smile as if I mean it. I can't let her and Jess down. "It's okay. I'm good."

"You're gonna be more than good, Nat. You're gonna be great. *We're* gonna be great." She puts her arm around my shoulders. I've known Harper only a week, but already she treats me like her best friend.

Still, I look to Jess—Jess and me and singing have gone together since grade one. "Harper's right," she says.

The pelicans in my stomach stop flapping so hard.

Applause. The Brassed-Off guys bow and come bouncing past us, high-fiving and fist-bumping one another. Harper rolls her eyes.

Darrell Bishop, the head of the camp, bounds out of the audience and onto the stage. The lights shine off his wire-framed glasses and perfectly bald head. "Was that not awesome?" he shouts. The audience claps.

He glances toward us, making sure we're ready. Jess pulls her guitar into position. Harper flashes a huge smile. She grabs my wrist and squeezes. I can't tell if it's to reassure me or to keep me from bolting.

Darrell gives us a thumbs-up and turns back to the audience. *Our* audience. "To finish off tonight's showcase of terrific young musicians, let's welcome to the stage three velvet-voiced gals. This trio couldn't agree on a name for their group"—the audience laughs, and Darrell raises one hand—"but that's okay, because they only came together this week, and hey, they sure find harmony when they sing. Ladies and gentlemen, I give you Harper Neale, Natalie Boychuk and Jess Lalonde."

Harper pulls me into the light. Jess follows close behind. Pelicans or not, it's time to sing.

Harper takes center stage behind the microphone, with me and Jess flanking her. We're tight together in a bright circle of light. It makes Jess's smooth black ponytail shine. Harper's caramel-colored skin seems to glow. I'm probably half-invisible beside them, all wispy blond hair and pale eyes.

Harper cozies up to the mic. "Fellow music geeks and gods," she starts, her voice silky, relaxed. At home. "I can't believe we've been together for only a week. It already feels...I don't know, like we're a family." She shades her eyes to look out at the other musicians, who have joined the audience. "Is that corny?"

"No!" they cheerfully yell.

Wow. Harper is only a year older than Jess and me—she's sixteen—but she can banter like a pro. Down in the front row, Darrell beams.

Harper smiles and nods. "Cool, cool. So, to keep this family-groove thing going, the girls and I have a song to share with you. Sound okay?"

The audience whistles and cheers. I quietly clear my throat and hope no one can hear my knees knocking together.

"Sweet," Harper says. She looks over to Jess, who smiles her easygoing smile as she strums the intro to "Four Strong Winds."

I take a breath, and we dive into the song.

I have to watch Harper's and Jess's mouths to make sure I stay in sync, see the cues for when to breathe. We worked hard on this all week, from the moment on Monday when Darrell discovered how our voices fit together to our pre-show rehearsal today.

I remember not to push the higher notes so they don't sound harsh. During the first chorus, Harper's fingers tap my back—a hint to move closer to her so our voices meld. My mouth dries out. So much to worry about. At least my knees have stopped shaking.

The second verse. Something shifts in me. The song takes over. Jess's voice is a deep current for Harper and me to sail on top of. It's suddenly easy to know when to breathe. I risk a look at the audience—smiling faces, a few people singing softly along. Everyone is together in the song. Nothing matters but all of us right here, right now, living the music. And my voice is helping to make this happen.

Too soon, the song ends. Jess's last chord vibrates in the air. Then, a beat of thick silence.

"Thank you," Harper murmurs into the mic.

Cheers break the spell. Relief washes over me like a sweet, cool shower, and I laugh.

I did it. I remembered the words, I got the harmonies, I didn't suck. I *performed*. I want to do this again. No, I *have* to do this again. I stand there, grinning, until Darrell waves us forward. "Take your bows!"

I practically fly to the front of the stage, and the clapping gets louder. Harper gets there next. She shoots me a dark look, freezing me for a second, then smiles out at the audience. Jess joins us. We all hold hands and bow. As the clapping dies down, Harper pulls her hand away and blows a kiss to the audience, triggering one last wave of applause.

"That's how it's done," she says so only I can hear, and she heads backstage.

Two

Jess and I step into the noisy after-party at Harper's grandma's house. For once I'm in a living room that's true to its name; it's full of life, crowded with paintings and posters and jumbled bookshelves. And our fellow musicians.

"Cool," Jess says. Her ultimate compliment.

We pick our way to an empty spot. On our left, the Chen sisters plunk out a piano duet. To our right, a violinist argues about rap versus hip-hop with a guy from Brassed-Off. I scope the room for Harper but don't see her. I can't shake the look she gave me before our bow.

"Did you talk to Harper after the performance?" I ask Jess.

"Nope. I saw Darrell talking to her, and then she left with her grandma."

"But you're sure we're still invited?" I picture Harper storming into the party, telling me to leave.

"Of course we're invited." Jess grabs a handful of chips from a bowl perched on top of the piano. "We *complete* her." She snorts.

Harper had said that in a rehearsal. I thought it was sweet, but it made Jess hoot with laughter. And *that* made Harper leave the room in a huff.

The Chen sisters finish their duet in a tangle of fingers and laughter.

"You have to admit, Harper was amazing tonight," I say.

Jess brushes off her chip-salty hands on her jeans. "She was good, Nat. We all were."

A tall red-headed guy squeezes past us with a banjo. Gabe Neufeld. I've been noticing him and his smile all week, and trying to get up the guts to talk to him. He wraps his plaid-shirted arm around a guy playing a harmonica in the dining room.

"I wish music camp wasn't ending," I say.

"Me too." Jess nods. "I will admit that."

Jess and I have just spent six fantastic days together, going to workshops and rehearsals during the day, singing together in her and her mom's apartment at night. Meanwhile, my parents and twelve-year-old brother, Eric, drove all over Manitoba to his hockey games. Tomorrow they come back, and I go home to endless hockey talk and stinky equipment bags. So much for my newfound life in music.

"Bandmates! Girlfriends!" Harper squeals as she comes toward us. Several heads turn. She's changed into red skinny jeans and a sequined top for the party.

"Group hug!" Harper grabs me and Jess. We're both pretty tall, so she only comes up to our chins.

I laugh, relieved that Harper isn't mad at me. But over the top of her curls, I see Jess grimacing. She's never been big on hugging. Sometimes I think Jess took up guitar just so she'd have a shield.

Harper lets go. "Welcome to *Casa de Musica*, aka Grandma Barb's place."

"It's nice she's letting us all invade." Jess straightens her T-shirt.

"She insisted! Gran's a music chick from way back." Harper points to a framed poster behind us.

Under swirly orange letters spelling out *Angels and Mortals* two bearded, long-haired dudes in jeans and fringed jackets; two women in floral dresses sit on wicker chairs. "That was her band in the sixties."

"Cool," I say, looking closer. "Which one is she?"

A warm voice behind me answers, "The one in the floppy hat, looking quite full of herself."

Grandma Barb in the flesh is short and slim, wearing faded jeans and a pink paisley blouse. A braid of brown hair threaded with gray drapes over one shoulder. "I grew out of that, thankfully." The corners of her eyes crinkle when she smiles.

"The hat?" I ask.

Harper laughs. "No, Nat. The being full of herself."

I feel myself turn red, but Grandma Barb takes my hand and says, "I do wish I still had that hat. Come on, let's get you girls something to eat. Performers are always starving after a show. Especially a show as good as yours."

Grandma Barb pulls me toward the crowded warmth of the kitchen. I'm happy to follow. *Performer.* She called me a performer.

* * *

The party's been going for a couple of hours. I sip from a big mug of tea with honey—"Good for the voice," Grandma Barb said—and listen to Gabe play a Sufjan Stevens song on his banjo.

"He's really good," I whisper to Harper, who's snug beside me on the living-room couch.

"You mean he's really cute," she whispers back.

I giggle. "You're really right." I'm drunk on tea and music.

Harper looks at me, wide-eyed. "Oh ho! Nat and Banjo Boy."

"Shut up!" I elbow her.

Jess gives us a "Shh!" look from across the room. Darrell's standing beside her, absorbed in Gabe's playing.

Darrell finally got to the party about ten minutes ago. Grandma Barb greeted him with a big hug and a beer. She taught him guitar when he was a kid, so Harper's known him forever.

Gabe finishes the song and says, "Thank you. Thank you very much," in a bad Elvis impersonation. It makes him even cuter.

I put down my tea to clap. Loudly.

Harper grabs a plate of oatmeal cookies from the coffee table. "I've heard the way to a banjo player's heart is through his stomach."

"Right. Heard that where, exactly?"

She pushes the plate at me. "Go!"

I take the cookies. "Okay, I will." I try to sound sassy. Performing tonight has made me braver. I step over kids sitting on the floor.

Gabe's talking with another guy when I reach him. "Hey, uh, nice song," I say to his back. So much for sassy.

He turns around, and there's that smile. That face. Cute hardly covers it.

"Pardon?" He slings his banjo over his shoulder. His glance shifts from me to the cookies.

I raise the plate. "The song you just played. It was great. The way you—"

"Thanks." He takes a cookie and is about to bite into it when he says, "For the compliment, I mean. And the cookie. Sorry—I'm so hungry." He pops the cookie into his mouth.

"I know! I was too. It's from performing." My alto voice has suddenly gone soprano on me. I watch Gabe chew.

He has really nice lips, full but not too full, and his cheeks are flushed as if he's come in from a walk in fresh air. His eyes are spring-leaf green. He swallows and gives me a polite nod. "Good cookie."

I'm staring. I'm a dork with a plate of cookies, watching a guy chew. I put the cookies down.

Before I can think of anything halfway intelligent to say, Darrell comes and shakes Gabe's hand. Jess appears, saying, "I should call my mom to pick us up, Nat."

"Already?" I'm Cinderella with the clock starting to toll midnight.

"Oh, hey, hang on," Darrell says. "I want to talk to you girls. Where's Harper?" He scans the room and waves her over.

What would Darrell need to tell us that he hasn't already? Did we do something wrong in the show? Jess doesn't look worried, but still...

Gabe says, "I should get going."

"Actually"—Darrell puts his hand on Gabe's shoulder—"I want to talk to you too."

Gabe and us. Now I can't tell if I'm nervous or excited.

Darrell grabs another beer and leads us to the closed-in front verandah. "It'll be quieter here."

Quieter and colder. March doesn't mean spring in Winnipeg. I rub my hands against my arms. Damp boots and shoes are piled by the door. We sit down on an old plaid couch. Darrell leans on the window ledge. Gabe's beside me, still holding his banjo.

Darrell takes a swig of beer. "You guys know you were good tonight, right? Really good."

Phew. We didn't do anything wrong.

Jess and Gabe and I glance at each other and shrug. Harper keeps her eyes focused on Darrell.

"Come on," he continues. "No false modesty. You were good. You've all got talent, you worked hard, you all rose to the challenge of performing."

Gabe says, "It's the first time I ever felt like a real musician."

"Bingo." Darrell leans forward and taps his knuckles against Gabe's banjo. "Now, you've all got a choice. You can go on taking lessons, maybe impressing your friends or your music teacher at school...whatever." He looks at the floor. Pauses. "Or you can ramp it up. Take things to the next level."

Inside me, the crazy pelicans are back. Jess stares at Darrell with the same expression she gets working out a difficult chord progression on her guitar. Darrell picks up his beer. Takes another slow swig. Puts down his beer. Looks at us.

"Argh! Come on, Darrell," Harper prompts. "The next level is?"

"I was waiting for someone to ask that." Darrell grins, pulls a piece of paper out of his shirt pocket and reads, "'The Young Performers contest gives teen musicians a chance to be part of the famous Tall Grass Music Festival. Contest winners will work with established musical mentors before performing at the festival itself.'" He looks up. "It could be a long shot, but—"

Harper leaps to her feet. "But we should totally go for it!"

I feel my mouth open, but nothing comes out. My insides swoop with happiness. Another chance for the trio to sing. For *me* to sing. On a real stage. At a real music festival. I spring up and grab on to Harper. We jump up and down like excited little kids.

I hear Gabe say, "That'd be amazing."

Darrell says, "Jess?" He sounds worried.

I stop Harper's bouncing. Jess sits still and quiet, regarding Harper. I don't expect crazy-excited from Jess, but calm-excited would be good.

"I'm going to go call my mom. It's late." Jess stands up, doesn't look me in the eye.

"But you're in, right?" I ask. The air in the verandah feels even colder than before.

"Maybe, Nat. I don't know." Jess walks into the house. I hear laughter and someone playing the violin inside. She closes the door behind her, and everything goes quiet.

Three

A meatball churns around in my brother's mouth as he talks. "Coach Tom says if I keep working my squeeze-and-score drills, I'll be unstoppable."

"He said you'd be hard to catch, Eric," Dad says, but he's smiling. He and Eric are like twins, except thirty years apart.

"Same thing." Eric finally swallows.

Mom shakes her head. "They are not the same thing."

"Whatever. They both mean I'm awesome."

The inspiring conversation of a sporting-goods store manager, an insurance agent and a preteen hockey nut.

I twist spaghetti onto my fork, but I'm hardly hungry. Yesterday at this time I was doing vocal warm-ups with Jess and Harper. Now I don't know if we'll ever sing together again.

All last night and this morning at her house, Jess never said a word about entering the contest. I couldn't make myself ask her. I was too afraid her answer would be no. But Harper's been texting—Yes from Jess yet?? Make her agree!!—and I haven't texted back.

"Are you trying to get your entire plate of spaghetti wrapped around that fork?" Mom holds her glass of wine and watches me, amused.

"I could do that." Eric stabs his fork into his spaghetti, twirling it.

I let my fork clatter onto the plate. "Not everything's a competition."

He shovels the fat forkful in and chews in my direction.

"Ugh! Mom..." I expect her to tell Eric to be civilized, but she's busy reading a text on her cell phone. Dad dishes up a second helping of spaghetti. Neither of them notices Eric. Or me.

I feel empty, as if the music camp, the show, the after-party never happened. I have to convince Jess to do the contest.

I push away from the table and head to the back door.

Mom calls, "Natalie! You haven't finished."

"I just remembered I left something at Jess's place that I need for school tomorrow." I yank on my boots and jacket. I leave my phone in the basket where we stash hats and gloves, so Mom—and Harper—can't reach me.

Outside, wet snow falls, making me shiver. Jess's apartment is a short block away, but it's long enough for the worries to pile up. What if she says no? If Jess won't do the contest, Harper doesn't need me. She's so good, she could enter it solo. Or she could even make a duo with Gabe. A street-light flickers out as I pass under it. I walk faster.

*　　*　　*

Jess sits cross-legged on her bed, cradling her guitar, sheet music spread out in front of her. She looks up when I come in but keeps fingerpicking a tune, like all she sees is the music in her head.

"That's nice. What is it?" I'm trying to ease my way toward what I have to ask.

Jess plays a few more bars. "'The Circle Game.' It's Joni Mitchell." She looks at the music. "Her tuning is genius, but super hard to do."

"You'll figure it out. You always do." I pull the chair away from Jess's desk. "Can I sit down?"

"Sure."

Beside me on the desk are tidy stacks of *Acoustic Guitar* magazine and a little pottery bowl filled with guitar picks. I stir my finger around in it. The picks make a teeth-chattering sound. "Did I say something wrong last night? At the party?"

"Wrong?" She glances at my finger in the bowl of picks.

I put my hands in my lap. "Something to make you mad?"

She says nothing.

"When we were all on the verandah?" Sometimes, talking to Jess feels like hard work.

She lays her guitar aside. "Oh. You mean when Harper declared that you and I could be backup singers in her quest for musical fame?" Her voice is cold.

"What?" A sour feeling opens in my gut. "We're not backup singers. That's not what Harper said."

"It's what she thinks." Jess's words come fast. "That dirty look she gave you at the show, when you were about to bow before she did? Lead-singer move."

So Jess saw it too. "Why didn't you say anything about that last night?"

"Not checking with us, not even *looking* at us, before announcing we'd enter the contest as a group? Lead-singer move."

"Harper just reacts fast. She's enthusiastic."

"Do you know why she was so 'fast' to jump on the contest idea?" Jess leans forward, hands on her knees. "Because she knew about it before we did. I could see it on her face when Darrell told us. He probably told her about it before last night."

"So? Why is that such a big deal?"

"Because she had it all planned out. Her way to get into the festival, with us making her sound good." A crease appears between Jess's dark eyebrows. "And you bounced right into her little plan. The two of you jumping up and down over a contest."

"I was excited." My eyes sting with tears.

She shakes her head. "It's a music festival, not a Miss Teen pageant. I want to be a musician, not a contestant. What about you?"

"I know I'm not a real musician like you. But I want to try." My voice is shaky.

Jess's face softens. "Nat."

"After the show I thought maybe I could be a musician, someday, with practice. But I felt like that because of how we sang together. All three of us." I wipe my eyes. "I thought you might have felt that too."

"I did. It was great on that stage." Jess's expression brightens but only for a second. "It's everything else around it that I hate."

The phone rings in the kitchen. "That's probably my mom," I say. "I ran out on dinner. I thought I'd throw up if I heard one more word about Eric's hockey."

"Did the little champion single-handedly win every game again?"

"Do *not* make me talk about it."

We laugh. It's a relief.

Jess's mom, Louise, knocks on the door. "Natalie, sweetie, your mom says it's time to come home. School night."

"Okay." As soon as Louise has left, I turn back to Jess. I can't avoid the question any longer. "So you don't want to be in the trio with Harper? We're not entering the contest?"

Jess looks at me and groans. But there's a hint of a smile.

I press on. "We probably won't even win. Darrell said it's a long shot, right? But entering would give us a chance to work with him more. He said that when you went inside, Jess. And you respect Darrell." I pick up the sheet music. "We could do this as one of our contest-entry songs. You always appreciate a musical challenge."

"Oh, boy." Jess raises her eyebrows, but her tone is jokey. "Did Harper write that speech for you?"

"It's not a speech. It's just me talking. You and me. We can handle Harper. Let her think we're backup singers. We know differently."

"*She* should know differently."

"She will. We'll show her."

"If you keep singing how you did last night, we will." Jess sounds calm again. More like herself.

"So we can be a trio? We're going to enter the contest?"

Jess gives an exaggerated sigh. "I guess we better come up with a name for this group."

I let out a whoop and hug her. She doesn't even seem to mind.

Four

I t's early Saturday morning at Darrell Bishop's
Music Land—DBML for short—one week
after the showcase. Jess and I sit on the vinyl
couch in Darrell's office. The room is plastered
with posters of everyone from Mozart to Lorde.
Jess tunes her already-tuned guitar.

Harper is late.

"I've got a lesson to teach at nine thirty."
Darrell taps out a syncopated beat with a pencil
on his Here Comes Treble coffee mug. "We won't
have much time if she doesn't get here soon."

Jess says nothing, but her tuning is an "I told
you so."

Harper was so excited last Sunday when I
phoned to tell her Jess said yes that she practically pierced my eardrum. "I'm calling Darrell

right now to set up our first session. This is going to be awesome!"

So how can she be late?

"Jess, why don't we do 'The Circle Game' for Darrell?" I sound like an awkward talk-show host, but it's better than Jess's stubborn silence.

Darrell stops his pencil solo. "You're thinking of that for your contest entry?"

"Maybe," Jess says, sounding suddenly doubtful. "I can do chords instead of picking. If you think that would be simpler."

"No, that's not the issue." Darrell seems about to say something, then changes his mind. "Go ahead. Do you need to retune for the song?"

Jess smiles. "No, I already practiced it first thing this morning. I was just making sure I was still tuned."

Once Jess decides to learn a song, she goes at it nonstop. To keep up, I've been singing along to videos of Joni Mitchell on my computer all week. Harper's soprano voice is closer to Joni's than mine is, so she should be the one singing the melody, but I'm not about to point that out right now.

Jess tucks her hair behind her ear, curves over her guitar and plays the intro. Just as I'm about to sing, footsteps clatter down the hallway. Harper appears at the office-door window, waving briskly. She bursts in, bringing along the scent of cold spring air.

"I am *so* sorry, you guys." She slings a tote bag off her shoulder and onto Darrell's desk and unwinds a long scarf from her neck. "I was Skyping with my parents and I lost track of time. By the way, they say hi, Darrell. They're on the road, on tour. They played Nashville and—"

Jess starts up on the guitar again, cutting Harper off. It flusters me, but Darrell doesn't say anything, so on my cue I start singing.

Harper listens for maybe ten seconds. "What are you doing?"

Jess stops playing.

"It's 'The Circle Game,'" I say.

"I know that." Harper sighs. "Everyone knows 'The Circle Game.'"

I didn't.

"Why are you singing it?"

Darrell says, "They're thinking of it for the contest entry."

"'They' are? 'They' didn't tell me." Harper perches on the arm of the couch. Jess shifts away.

"It wasn't a big plan or anything." I glance from Harper to Darrell. "It's just that Jess had been working on it. Then when you were late—"

"Because if anyone had bothered to ask me," Harper interrupts, "I would have said we shouldn't do it."

Great. The song I used to convince Jess to join the trio is one Harper hates.

"Interesting. Why not?" Darrell crosses his arms. "Beautiful, classic tune. Opportunities for good harmonies."

"A classic means six other groups will do it. And actually? It's too girly. Too folk princess-y."

Darrell stays silent. I think he agrees with Harper.

Beside me, Jess looks ready to spit. "Folk princess-y? You're calling Joni Mitchell, one of the best musicians ever, male or female, girly?"

"Not her. The song. Dragonflies, painted ponies, carousels." Harper waves her hands, dismissive. "We don't need to be so old school. So folk."

Jess thrusts her chin forward. "Isn't the Tall Grass a folk festival?"

"Not really," Harper says. "Have you been to Tall Grass, Jess? Or any music festival?"

"No." Jess sounds calm, but her fingers tighten their grip on her guitar.

Harper smirks. "I've been to every Tall Grass since I was born. Actually, since before I was born."

Darrell shifts impatiently in his chair. "I've got about five minutes."

"You guys," I say.

Harper plows ahead. "You think I'm exaggerating, Jess? My mom was pregnant with me when she and my dad performed there. Ever hear of the Desmond Neale Band?"

Jess smiles. "Nope."

"Right. 'Cause you know so much about music."

"Harper!" It's like the only way to keep the trio together is to keep Jess and Harper apart. "Jess worked hard on 'The Circle Game.' Can't you give it a chance?"

Harper shrugs. "Just because you worked hard on something doesn't mean it's the right thing to do. In music you don't get A's for effort."

"Do you get F's for being late?" Jess strums a sour chord.

"Right." Darrell pushes up out of his chair. "I've kept quiet because I wanted to give the three of you a chance to show me how you can work together. Unfortunately, you have."

"Unfortunately?" My voice shakes. My pulse thrums a bass beat in my neck.

"You have talent. I'd love to help you put together a solid CD to enter the Young Performers contest. But my time is always tight, so the time we do get together has to be productive. Or I won't do it."

Darrell never sounded this stern during the whole of March break. It's enough to silence Jess and Harper.

But he hasn't totally shut the door on us—yet.

"How can we prove we're worth working with?" I force myself to sound confident.

Darrell takes a file folder off his desk. "I'd picked out some potential songs, hoping we'd go through them together today. Why don't you take them and come back to me in a week with your choices."

Harper reaches past me to take the folder.

"How many songs do we need for the CD?" I ask.

"Two." Darrell drains his coffee. "Do you think you can agree on two whole songs?"

"Of course." Harper forces a laugh.

Jess puts her guitar back into its case and says nothing.

"I hope so." Darrell gestures toward his office door. "See you next week."

"Thanks, Darrell," I say. "You won't be disappointed."

I hope.

Five

Out on the street, I pull on my mitts. "Let's find somewhere warm to look through those songs. Harper, you know the neighborhood. Where's a good spot?"

"Actually, I'm heading home," Jess says, hitching her guitar case onto her shoulder. "Essay due for English."

Harper, in the middle of wrapping her scarf, drops her hands. "Stop walking out on us!"

Jess faces her. "Stop telling me what to do!"

I want to shake them both. "Didn't you guys hear what Darrell said?"

"You're right." Harper composes herself. "I'm sorry, Jess. 'The Circle Game' could be fine."

"It's not about the song. I can do other songs." Jess stands close to Harper, so Harper has to look up at her. "I've taken guitar since I was seven. I've been in choirs for nine years. I've studied a lot of music. So don't treat me like some know-nothing."

Harper backs away. "Okay. Sheesh."

"I'm sure she didn't mean you're a know-nothing," I say.

Jess shoots me an "Oh, please!" look.

I ignore it. "Where can we go, Harper?"

She snaps her fingers. "Hang on." She pulls her phone out of her bag and turns away, texting.

Jess stares down at the sidewalk, her chin tucked into her coat collar. At least she's not leaving. I say nothing, hoping that'll keep her fastened to the spot.

Harper turns back to us. "Come on. Grandma Barb to the rescue."

*   *   *

Up in the slanted-ceiling attic of her house, Grandma Barb sets a tray of sandwiches and lemon water on an ottoman. "This room has strong musical karma. You'll see." She straightens up, tossing her braid over her shoulder. The room is a sunny yellow and has a keyboard and a wall-mounted rack of five guitars. A turntable sits on a shelf crammed with vinyl records.

"Thanks," Jess says. She and I are both tucked up in chairs facing the ottoman. Harper sits cross-legged on a sheepskin rug beside it.

"We could use some good karma," I add.

Grandma Barb smiles. "Arguments happen all the time in bands. They're part of the process. People argue because they care. You'll get used to it." She reaches down and gives Harper's shoulder a squeeze before heading back downstairs.

I can't imagine getting used to arguments.

"She is so cool, Harper," Jess says. "First with the after-party and now letting us use her music room."

Harper looks up from the pile of sheet music Darrell gave us. "She is."

It's the first thing they've agreed on today. The three of us eat in silence for a few minutes. Then Harper brushes crumbs from her lap and takes the sheet music across the room to sit at the keyboard. "Okay, lightning round. I'll say the song, you guys say yes or no. Go with your gut instinct. No hard feelings."

"Sounds good to me," Jess says, pulling her guitar out of its case.

I give a thumbs-up, still swallowing some sandwich.

Harper takes the top song off the pile. "'Eight Days a Week.' Hey, yeah. Lots of good harmonies in that."

I scrunch up my nose. "The Beatles. That's practically the only band my dad likes. And he has zero interest in music."

"So that's a no?" Jess tilts her head at me as she strums the song chords.

I shrug, like it's a food allergy I can't help.

Harper raises her eyebrows. "Interesting." She tosses the Beatles onto the floor. "Next up. 'Dreams.' Fleetwood Mac." She presses the music to her chest. "I love this song. So awesome."

"So old. So hippie," Jess says.

"Gee, tell us what you really think." Harper's face clouds over.

"No hard feelings," I remind them.

Silence.

Harper smiles and drops "Dreams" to the reject pile.

I let out my breath.

She pulls out the next song. "'Scarborough Fair,' by Simon and Garfunkel. Well, it's not exactly *by* them."

"It's not?" I remember listening to the song in a grade-five music class, Mrs. Duchamp holding up a faded album cover showing two geeky guys in turtlenecks.

"It's an old English ballad. Simon and Garfunkel just did their own arrangement of it." Harper plays the first few bars.

"It is super pretty," I say.

"But you don't want to get too folky," Jess reminds Harper. "That's so folky we'd have to wear medieval maiden dresses and fling daisies around."

"We'd look awesome in medieval maiden dresses," I joke.

"Uh, no." Jess gives a thumbs-down.

"Speaking of maidens," I say, "any women in that bunch?"

"Good point." Harper flips through the pile. "Tegan and Sara...Feist...guy...guy...the Civil Wars—they're a girl and guy. But their harmonies are incredible."

"They're amazing," Jess says. "Have you seen their videos? They're practically joined at the lungs. I'd do one of their songs." She joins Harper by the keyboard.

"Me too." Harper reads the song title—"I've Got This Friend"—and hums some notes.

I don't want to say it, but I have to. "I've never heard of them."

Harper and Jess look over at me, and my face goes hot. I'm always the one who knows the least about music. I feel antsy thinking and talking about songs—I just want to sing.

I push up out of the chair. "Let's try it."

"Yes!" Harper gives me a high five. "Jess and I can sing it through once to give you a feel for it."

Jess adds, "You've got a good ear. You'll pick it up quickly." She leans over Harper's shoulder to peer at the music. "So, key of D." She puts her capo onto the guitar neck. "You sing the melody?"

"Yeah. Without keyboard. I think it'll work better with just a guitar. You'll love the opening riff." Harper pushes the music closer to Jess.

They look totally comfortable, two band members figuring out stuff together. I roll my shoulders, trying to relax myself into belonging.

Jess starts picking. Harper's voice comes in sweet but strong. She has an easy way of singing that only comes from tons of practice. Harper could probably sing before she could talk. I'm just starting out on a road she's walked her whole life.

When Jess joins in, her voice has a warmer tone than Harper's but with an edge. Even when we were little, starting in choir, Jess sounded older than the other kids. Like she'd figured out more.

Jess plays the guitar solo in the middle of the song and I snap myself back to attention. I can't quite hear where I fit in the mix. I try coming in for the last verse at least, but stop when my harmonies wobble. Harper and Jess continue without me, their heads bobbing in time.

When they finish, Jess says, "Pretty good."

Harper hoots. "Pretty good? Darrell has to love this. We'll slay him with our chops."

Jess looks skeptical. "Our chops?"

Harper gives her a friendly little push. "Come on. You know what I mean."

"That can be our band name," I say. "Slayed With Chops." I do some cheesy air guitar, hoping no one mentions my off-pitch harmony.

Jess laughs. "Uh, you keep working on that, Nat."

"Songs first, band name later," Harper says. "Let's go again. We need to break down the parts." We set to work. A real trio. Finally.

Six

arrell's eyes are closed. "It'll help me listen better," he told us before we started the song. It's a little weird, as if Jess and Harper and I are singing our hearts out while he naps.

But a little weird is okay. Because everything else feels better than it did a week ago. Even the sunshine and melting snow outside seem to reflect our moods.

When we finish, Darrell's eyes pop open. "Nice. Good work on the fingering, Jess. We'd have to fix the balance of your voices. The tempo was uneven too." He must notice we're drooping, because he spreads his arms wide and smiles. "But I can tell you've worked hard on it. I'd love to help you put together your Tall Grass entry."

"Yes!" Harper thrusts her fist up in the air. "Slayed!"

"What?" Darrell asks.

"Inside joke." I laugh. "We're pumped."

"Pumped is good. Working as a team is even better."

"Oh, we're a team now." Harper wraps her arm around my shoulder. Jess looks content as she tucks her guitar into its case.

Darrell says he has a student waiting, so we sort out a time to come back for a full session.

"In the meantime, keep practicing," he says as we all head down the narrow hallway. "I assume you girls have picked out a second song too."

My eyes dart to Jess. Jess's eyes dart to Harper, who says, "Um..."

Agreeing on one song seemed to use up our week's supply of agreeing. It's part of the process I kept reminding myself every time an argument threatened to break out.

"We're narrowing down our choices," I say.

Luckily, Darrell is too distracted to ask for specifics. "Great. Go for up-tempo."

"Up-tempo. Yes," Harper says.

Outside, we do a happy dance. Or at least Harper and I do, but Jess doesn't seem to mind this time.

*   *   *

After school the following Monday, I take a bus downtown to a music store a pianist at the after-party raved about: "It's so totally *not* a chain store." I want to find a second number for the contest, to prove to Harper and Jess that I can contribute more to the trio.

I'm only a few blocks from DBML, but the neighborhood is a different, funkier world. I stroll past old factory buildings turned into vintage shops and hipster bars. I hear "Passing on your left!" and a guy in black jeans and tartan Doc Martens zips past me on a skateboard, a trumpet case strapped to his back. I round a corner and see the sign hanging from a brick building: Crescendo Music.

Inside the heavy wooden door, a staple-stabbed bulletin board is cluttered with band posters and ads for used instruments. I spot a poster for the Tall Grass festival. I'm walking into my future.

The tall-windowed space is crammed with books, CDs and DVDs. Mellow jazz flows from the sound system. Anchoring everything is a counter topped with a curled-up gray cat. Behind the cat, a middle-aged guy with a ponytail and the bushiest beard I've ever seen looks up from a magazine.

"Help you find anything?" His voice is so deep I think I feel the floorboards vibrate.

I shift my backpack. "I'm looking for music."

"Pretty sure we've got some of that." Bushy-Beard chuckles, the sort of guy who cracks himself up.

I smile politely. "I mean sheet music."

"Voice or instrument?"

"Both. Voice and guitar. It's for my trio." *My* trio. Saying that sends a thrill of happiness through me.

"Okeydokey." He lumbers over to a shelf full of labeled drawers. I follow, aware of other customers silently browsing the store—all the non-newbies who don't need help.

"What's your thing?" Bushy-Beard asks. "We've got rock, pop, blues, country, jazz, folk, Celtic, world, alternative. And that's just the easy-to-label stuff."

"I guess, uh, not folk, exactly. But not too pop either. Something upbeat," I add, remembering Darrell's suggestion.

"Upbeat, but no Peter, Paul and Mary, and no Katy Perry." The guy opens a drawer. "Indie singer-songwriter?"

"Sure." I let my backpack drop to the floor and lean in to see if I recognize any of the musicians' names.

A voice behind me says, "You looking for songs for the Tall Grass contest?"

Gabe.

"Hey!" I squeak, like he's sprung from a jack-in-the-box. I clear my throat. "Yeah, I am."

"So the trio's still together? Your friend's on board?"

Right. He was there when Jess walked out of the after-party.

"Jess. She is."

"Glad she came around." Gabe's banjo case hangs over his left shoulder. I wonder if he goes everywhere with it, the way Jess does with her guitar. "You three are natural together."

"Now if we could only agree on what songs to sing."

"I guess that's the plus of being a solo act—easy to get mine picked out. Darrell told me to get this." He holds up a yellow, spiral-bound book called *Splitting the Licks*.

"He's helping you too?" I picture Gabe in Darrell's studio with the trio. Me singing, Gabe watching, Gabe strumming, me watching...

"Yeah. Thank goodness."

"I know, right? I mean, not that you need help. Just, I'm glad he's helping us. The trio."

"Got it." Gabe grins.

"Excellent choice for five-string," Bushy-Beard rumbles, leaning across me to tap on Gabe's banjo book. I'd forgotten he was there. "You kids trying for the Young Performers gig?"

"Yep." Gabe pushes his shoulders back, all confident-looking. "Nat here is in a fantastic trio. Sweet three-part harmonies. They'll get in for sure."

He remembered my name. I feel myself blush. "Nothing's for sure," I say.

"Lots of stellar acts got their start with the Young Performers. Including yours truly." Bushy-Beard pats his chest. "Yes indeedy..." His eyes get a faraway look.

Before he can drift into a full-on memory trip, a little bell dings at the counter. The cat leaps down and scoots behind a shelf. A woman with spiky blond hair and a stack of books looks impatiently our way.

"Yikes, I can't keep her waiting if I value my life." Bushy-Beard gives Gabe a hearty thump on the back. "You seem to know your stuff, buddy. Maybe you can help your friend here find some music. No Katy Perry though." He winks and does an awkward trot back to the cash desk.

Gabe readjusts his dislodged banjo case. "Wow. The Young Performers contest must be mighty old if that dude was in it."

A loud laugh escapes me before I clamp my hand over my mouth.

Gabe looks sideways at me. He nods, mock-serious. "That was a little rude of me, wasn't it?"

I hold his look, return the nod. "It was." After a pause I add, "I bet he had the same ponytail back then—"

"And beard!"

Bushy-Beard glances over, which makes us giggle. Somehow, Gabe sounds good even when he giggles.

I have to focus. "I better get some songs."

"Right." Gabe snaps his fingers. "There are tons of songbooks this way." He heads toward another section of the store.

I pick up my backpack and follow. Gabe's long-legged stride makes his banjo case bump lightly against his back.

"You don't need to help me just because the guy said to."

Gabe looks over his shoulder. "I'm happy to."

I'm flat-out happy.

Seven

About an hour later, Mom, still in her work clothes, grills me for getting home late. Apparently it's the end of the world that the lasagna wasn't shoved into the oven right at 4:45. I spot Eric past her shoulder, gleefully tossing the salad. He just wants to hear Mom get mad at me.

"Eric was home," I point out. "Can't he open an oven?"

Mom's eyebrows arch. "Natalie—"

"I was doing math homework," Eric says.

"As if!"

"Natalie." Mom crosses her arms. "The point is, it was your responsibility and you shirked it to go shopping."

Like I was getting designer shoes. "I had to get music for the trio."

I don't mention Gabe. He had just asked me to have coffee with him when Mom nag-called my cell, telling me to come home.

Eric swans past, saying, "Ooh, the trio" in a snooty voice.

Mom sighs. "Eric, go do your math homework."

He skulks out of the kitchen. Mom turns away to pour herself a glass of wine. Maybe she's finished with me. I'm inching out of the room when she says, "When is this music thing anyway?"

This music thing. She's as bad as Eric. "I told you before. The Tall Grass festival's in July. But the contest CD is due in less than two weeks. We need to practice the songs." The new songbook practically burns a hole in my backpack. I want to get to my room to devour it.

Mom drops into a chair and slides her cell phone onto the table. She rubs her eyes. "Are you sure you want to do this contest?"

"What? Yes." Would she ever ask Eric if he's sure he wants to play hockey?

"It seems to take up a lot of your time for..." She shakes her head.

It hits me. "You don't think we'll get in."

She gives me a pained look. "I'm no expert on music contests, but I'd guess the odds are long. You're new to this singing-in-a-trio stuff. Usually it's the exceptional ones who—"

"Why are other people always the exceptional ones? Maybe we're exceptional."

"I'm sure you girls are good." Not that she's heard us. "And music can be a lovely hobby, but it can't be everything."

I hear the garage door grinding open, Dad's car pulling in after another thrilling day at Sport Zone.

I want to yell, "Is this everything? Boring, exhausting jobs, and lasagna, and nagging your kids?"

But Mom would blow up. I need her to let me keep practicing. I take a deep breath. "Okay, sorry. I won't be late again. Anyway, you're right, we probably won't get into the festival and that'll be that."

Saying this feels like pulling my heart out of my mouth.

Before Mom can give me any more depressing parental wisdom, her phone vibrates on the table. She straightens up and answers, "Sandra Boychuk."

I stare at her talking about some insurance policy. The well-trained worker bee.

She's never felt the magic of being onstage. Of giving her voice, her self, over to a song. To something bigger than herself. All of the things I discovered at the music camp with Harper and Jess.

Mom's wrong. Music *can* be everything.

My songbook is out of my backpack before I even close my bedroom door.

* * *

The next morning I meet Jess at our usual corner to walk to school. It's a bright but still-cold day. I'm buzzy from too much coffee. I stayed up super late with the songbook. It was so worth it.

"I might have found our second song." I open the book and hand it over.

"'Blue Skywriting,'" Jess reads. "Do I know this?"

"The band's called Electric Daisy Chain."

She wrinkles her nose. "That doesn't help."

"Just look it over."

Jess scans the song, her eyes brightening. I wish I could read music the way she and

Harper can. They instantly hear what they read. I try, but then I have to plunk everything out on our ancient piano. Kind of tricky at one thirty in the morning.

Jess taps the page. "This could be nice, Nat."

"Nice?" I fling up my hands. "Is that you being excited?"

"*Really* nice?" Jess teases. She hands the book back as we wait to cross an intersection. "Has Harper heard it?"

"No. I wanted to show you first. You don't think she'll go for it?"

"No, I think she should."

"Yes! I was hoping you'd think so." I found a song. I *do* know good music.

"Yeah. The melody line is right in her range." The light changes, and Jess sets off ahead of me.

"Oh. That's good." I don't mention that I was hoping to do the melody, that I thought it'd be perfect for me. Harper's already doing the melody for the other song.

Jess and I join the stream of kids trooping up the steps. She says, "Let's go over it at lunch. We can steamroll Harper with it later, and she'll have to agree."

As if Harper wouldn't agree to getting the lead vocals again.

*　*　*

At Jess's place after school, we sing "Blue Skywriting" for Harper over the computer, to save the long bus ride to her place. Harper says, "Nat, you are a total genius. Total. I can't believe I've never heard that song before. I love it!" She puts her hand up to her monitor as if to fist-bump us.

"So, you think it'll work as a second song?" I ask, fist-bumping back.

"Absolutely." She nods rapidly. "As long as I do the melody."

Jess leans her head close to mine. "That's the direction we were going in."

I stay quiet. Smile my "everything's great" smile.

Harper makes a happy-pouty face. "Aww, you guys are the best."

"We are," Jess cheerfully answers. She knocks her foot against my leg, well out of camera range.

I knock back. We've got our two songs. I just wish Jess and Harper thought this one was perfect for me.

Eight

Another Saturday at Darrell Bishop's Music Land, this time in the downstairs studio. It is a cocoon of quiet—padded walls, no windows, rugs layered on the floor. We slide headphones over our ears, and I feel like we're astronauts pulling on helmets. We've been rehearsing in Grandma Barb's attic for over a week, since Harper went for my song choice. Now we're ready for blastoff.

Darrell's voice lands right in my ears. "Can everybody hear me okay?"

Jess and Harper nod.

"Loud and clear," I say. I've promised myself to be confident today, to try to be as capable as Harper and Jess. I want to show Darrell he was right to have faith in the trio. In me.

He sits in the control booth, separated by a large soundproof window from the "live" room where Jess, Harper and I arrange ourselves around a single mic. We line our toes up with three strips of green tape marking our spots on the floor.

"Shouldn't we have our own mics?" Harper asks. She's in the center, with Jess and me on either side, facing each other. "It feels crowded."

Jess's eyes catch mine. *Here she goes again.*

Darrell shakes his head. "We'll be aiming for a real simple recording, Harper. No separate tracks for each voice or for Jess's guitar. No reverb." His tone is mellow but businesslike. "The judges want to hear you nice and unadorned."

Jess, tuning her guitar, says, "We might have only one mic at the festival, Harper."

"I know that. I was just checking."

"One thing, guys?" I wait until they're both looking at me. "We haven't actually gotten *into* the festival yet."

Their mouths drop open.

"Listen to us!" Harper presses her palm against her forehead. "Talking as if it's a done deal. I bet that's super bad luck."

Darrell laughs. "Don't worry. You're feeling positive. That's good." He rolls his chair back to take a sip of coffee well away from all of the sound controls. "So you've picked a second song? Should we start with that?"

"Definitely," Harper jumps in. "'Blue Skywriting.' An undiscovered gem."

"Discovered by Nat," Jess adds.

"No kidding?" Darrell looks approvingly at me. "You found something your picky bandmates could agree on?"

"Hey!" Harper puts her hands on her hips.

Jess laughs.

"Now we just have to convince you," I say to Darrell. It better be an easy sell. We don't have time to argue over more songs.

"Let's hear it," Darrell says. "Treat this as a regular rehearsal. The mic and headphones are there so you can get used to them and I can hear how you sound. We'll record tomorrow."

His words trigger a flutter of nerves in me, but the good kind. We're really doing this.

The song has a tricky start—no intro chords, no easing into it. The first verse launches with Jess's power strumming and Harper singing,

"*Out of the blue / that's where you found me / Wrote your love in full view / said you had to astound me.*"

Jess's strumming steps us up to the chorus. She sings, "*With your blue skywriting.*" I layer over top with "*Bright blue skywriting,*" and Harper joins in, singing, "*Blue skywriting.*" Then Jess and I cut out and Harper ends with "*swept me away.*"

We continue on through the second verse and chorus, then the bridge and right to the end. Jess floats the final chord off her strings.

Darrell nods at us through the window. "Good job."

Harper bounces lightly on the balls of her feet. "Isn't it cool how the chorus takes off?" Her voice is revved and impatient, ready to keep going.

"That is cool," Darrell agrees. He pulls off his glasses and rubs his eyes.

Harper and Jess and I exchange looks. Doesn't he like the song? He has to like it. We stand extra still, like we'll break something if we move.

I finally ask, "What do you think, Darrell?"

He puts his glasses back on, takes us in. "Great song. Good choice, Nat."

I let out a breath. Everyone likes the song I picked. Jess holds her hand up to me for a high five.

"Can I hear it again?" Darrell goes on. "But with you doing the melody?"

"The lead part?" I blink. My heart speeds up. "Me?"

"Yep," he says. Simple as that.

Harper looks like Darrell's speaking a foreign language. "Uh..." Her mouth clamps shut, stunned.

"Sure," I say and feel something inside me lift up. A window opening, letting in air.

"Sweet," Jess says.

Harper shakes off her silence. "Don't expect much. We haven't rehearsed it that way."

She may not have, but I worked on the melody line the first night I found the song and every night after the trio practiced.

Darrell leans back and takes another sip of coffee. "Give it a whirl. Rehearsals are for playing around with sounds. I'm not looking for perfection."

"I am," Harper says under her breath, but of course it's loud and clear to us. "Hang on."

She takes off her headphones. Back turned, she makes a show of grabbing a bottle of water off a table, taking several sips and stretching her neck.

While Harper's unplugged from us, Jess says, "I think you doing the melody is a great idea, Nat. I wish I'd thought of it."

I wish she had too, but that's okay now.

I concentrate on feeling loose and ready. I breathe slowly in and out, looking down at my toes touching that green tape line. I have to sing this song better than Harper did if I want the melody part to be mine.

Then Harper's voice invades my headphones. "What's Banjo Boy doing here?"

I look up and see Gabe, his army jacket and jeans spotted with rain, standing inside the control-room door. So much for my attempt to stay loose and relaxed. Is he going to watch us—me—sing?

Darrell says, "You're early, man," though he doesn't sound annoyed. He and Gabe do the handshake, shoulder-grab, guy-greeting thing.

"Aww, look." Harper puts her hand to her heart with fake sincerity. "Best buds. Taking up our studio time."

Jess points to our mic and whispers, "They can hear us."

Harper shrugs. "It's okay. Nat's Banjo Boy's biggest fan."

"Harper!" I cover the mic.

Her brown eyes go all wide and innocent.

In the control booth, Gabe doesn't seem to have heard us. He's taking his banjo case off his shoulder, looking for a spot to set it down.

Darrell's back in his chair. "Girls, would you mind if Gabe sits in on the rehearsal? He's early for his recording session, and it's good to see how fellow musicians work. It's entirely up to you though."

Gabe leans down to Darrell's mic. "You're welcome to watch me record after. It'd help me, having an audience."

When Gabe and I were at Crescendo Music and he told me he was working with Darrell, this was exactly what I wanted to happen. Now my throat tightens up, my mouth goes dry. What if I tank the melody?

"I'm cool with him staying," Jess says.

"Whatever. Fine," Harper says. "Unless you're uncomfortable with it, Nat."

Right. She's the relaxed pro. I'm the nervous rookie.

"No. Of course you can stay, Gabe." I try for an easygoing smile. It feels like a too-tight guitar string.

But he smiles back. "Sweet. Thanks."

Darrell claps his hands together. "Great. Back to the top of 'Blue Skywriting.' Jess, why don't you play a few bars so Nat can hear the melody first?"

"No need. I'm good." I can't let Harper think I'm not ready for this. I wipe my suddenly wet palms against my jeans. I look to Jess and she nods a silent count-in. I start to sing.

It's strange to hear myself, alone, through the headphones. I feel a quaver in my voice off the top and expect Darrell to stop me. But he's got his eyes closed, listening the way he did when we all sang in his office. I avoid looking at Gabe.

We get through the first verse and chorus and are starting the second verse when Harper stops. She steps back from the mic, shaking her head.

"What's up?" Darrell asks.

"You don't hear that?" Harper replies. "I'm off. I keep shifting back down into the melody. It's what I'm used to."

I say, "I thought you sounded—"

"Sorry." Harper takes a restraining hold on my arm. "Can you let Darrell deal with this?"

"Okay." Mortified, I focus only on Darrell.

His eyebrows pull together. "It was slightly off, but you found your way again quickly." He shrugs. "Nothing to worry about. Let's get through the song once, and then we'll go back to any rough spots."

Harper lets out a little grunt of frustration and flashes a glare my way, but she comes back to position.

We start again. Harper stops after the first chorus. So I stop too. Jess keeps going, strumming hard, singing the low harmony with a forced smile.

"Earth to Jess," Harper hisses, too close to the mic. Jess ignores her.

In the control booth, Darrell has his hands up in a "What is happening?" way. Gabe leans back, arms crossed and a wry smile on his face. Yeah, we're pretty entertaining. At this rate, we'll never be ready to record tomorrow.

Darrell leans forward. "Can. We. Please. Focus."

That stops Jess. "Sorry."

"Thank you. Yes," Harper says, as if she wasn't the one derailing us. "I'm still not feeling the harmony part, Darrell."

He sighs, pushes his chair back and rubs his head. Gabe looks down, like we're an accident he should avert his eyes from.

My stomach's a churning pool of anxiety. I can't spend the day as Harper's target. And we need to get the songs perfect for tomorrow. "Darrell, can I go back to singing the harmony?"

I sense Harper staring at me, alert as a hunting dog. And I'm the duck, dropping at her feet.

Jess groans. "Nat, don't be a—"

"If she's not comfortable with the melody," Harper interrupts, "I think we should respect that."

"Oh, that is hilarious," Jess says.

"Listen up, girls." Darrell leans in to the mic, his voice firm. "Nat, you can manage the melody. I need to hear more before I decide who should do it for the recording."

"But Darrell," Harper starts.

"Harper." He levels his eyes at her. "You should know musicians need to be flexible and professional. Everything we do is in service to the song."

"Got it." For once, Harper's voice sounds small.

"Good." Darrell checks his watch, smiles at us. "Let's try this again."

Jess cracks her knuckles. "Gladly."

In service to the song. I like that. I glance at Gabe and find he's leaning forward, head cupped in his hands, smiling at me.

I breathe in deeply and take it from the top again.

*   *   *

The fourth time Harper skews the harmony enough to throw off the melody, I know I have to give in. Frustration is creeping into my voice, and there's a tightness in my chest making the high notes feel just out of reach. "Darrell, I'm sorry. I can't do this."

His lips are pinched together as he considers me through the control-room glass. I'm pretty sure he's fed up with how long our session is taking. But he's still silent. So is Jess. Harper, I'm guessing, is cheering to herself.

"You sure?" Darrell says.

I notice Gabe shaking his head—*Don't do it, Nat*—but I know Harper's not going to give up. "I'm sure."

Harper wraps her arms around me in a stifling hug. She says something, but we're away from the mic, so I have to pull my headphones off to hear her properly. "It's okay," she says sweetly. "The melody's tough in this song. You've made the right decision."

Fighting off the urge to shove Harper aside, I peel away from her. "Thanks." I don't trust myself to say anything else. I put my headphones back on, ready to rehearse the song one more time.

At least I know I can nail harmony. Unlike Harper.

Nine

ater that afternoon, I stir sugar into my tea while Gabe waits for his latte at the counter. We're in the Honeycomb Café, across the street from Crescendo Music. Nearby, a guy slouches over a muffin and a paperback. A gray-haired woman types on a laptop, her long-empty coffee mug pushed aside. Rain patters against the window beside me. The place oozes mellow vibes. I could do with some mellowing, after the way things went in the studio.

"I think we have totally earned this sucker." Gabe arrives with a giant cinnamon bun on a plate. "Say you'll help me eat it."

"Just try to stop me." I pull off a chunk and pop it in my mouth.

"Excellent." He does the same. We both chew away like our bodies are starved for cinnamon and sugar.

Between mouthfuls, Gabe says, "I still can't believe you let Harper take the melody in that song."

I try to sound casual. "She's a fantastic singer."

"So are you. But you don't try to make your bandmates sound bad so you get the lead vocal."

"Let's talk about something else."

I want to stop worrying about the trio. I want to get to know Gabe. I point to the case sitting at his feet like a faithful dog. "Let's talk about banjos."

"Seriously?" His smile tells me he'd *love* to talk about banjos.

"Seriously. You're the only banjo player I know. Guys usually go for guitars."

"I started with the guitar. I still play. Jess rocks at it, by the way."

"She does." I suspect she's better than Gabe, but I don't say so. "Now, banjos. Go."

Gabe grins and leans back, his long legs stretched out. They almost touch mine. I hold very still. "My dad took me to the Tall Grass festival a few summers ago and we saw this dude playing banjo there and, I don't know, I just loved the sound."

"The banjo sound."

He nods. "I loved the whole day. People hanging out in the sun, happy and dancing. Being together. The banjo sounded exactly the way that day felt."

Gabe gazes out the window, but I can tell he's not seeing the view. I wish I was with him on that Tall Grass day. I let my foot shift so it touches his. He doesn't move away.

"I taught myself at first, and then I found Darrell. I keep playing to hang on to the feeling of that day. To get myself back to Tall Grass. Onstage." Gabe takes a drink and wipes his knuckles across his mouth. A thrum of warmth ripples through me.

"That's so awesome." I try to think of something deeper to say. A gurgly hiss from the espresso machine fills the silence.

Gabe taps the table and leans forward. "And except for my dad, no one else knows my nerdy banjo story. So now I'm going to have to kill you."

I laugh. "Darn."

"Price you pay for asking about banjos."

I love the idea of knowing something about Gabe that no one else knows. I lean forward too. "I think you're right about how banjos sound. I loved hearing you play today."

"Thanks." Gabe's cheeks redden. He's a blusher, same as me. "Okay, your turn."

"My turn what?"

"Your turn to share some deep, dark, nerdy truth about yourself."

"What if I don't have a nerdy truth?" I sip some tea.

"Impossible. Every musician does. Tell me, or I get this last hunk of cinnamon bun." He reaches for it.

"Hey!" I pull the plate to my side of the table. "Okay. I do have a nerdy truth. Brace yourself."

Gabe cradles his latte. "Is it very nerdy?"

"Very." I can't believe I'm sharing this with a guy I'm crushing on. "I'm an excellent whistler. My grandpa taught me. He won contests."

"Whistling?" Gabe rubs his hands together greedily. "I am *so* going to need a demonstration!"

I look around the café. Paperback guy is gone. Typing lady is still typing, ignoring everything, including the fresh espresso steaming beside her. The tattooed and well-pierced girl behind the counter is talking on her cell.

"Here goes. This was his favorite song." I lick my lips and launch into "The Dock of the Bay," complete with the fancy, birdlike trills Grandpa loved.

Gabe's eyes go wide and he breaks into a huge smile.

I can't help smiling back. Which kills the whistle.

"Hey! Don't stop," he says, reaching down to his banjo case.

"It's impossible to whistle and smile at the same time!" I say, laughing.

He straightens, banjo at the ready. "Okay, I'll be serious." He shifts his chair so we're facing each other, no table in the way. "Go ahead."

I start again and Gabe joins in with the banjo. He does look serious, his green eyes focused on mine as if he's reading the notes there. When we get to the end, he makes the last chord vibrate until my whistling dies away. Our eyes stay locked together.

There's clapping. "Omigod, you guys are the cutest!" It's the girl behind the counter. "You should be at, like, the Tall Grass festival. Have you heard of it?"

"Oh yeah," Gabe answers. He turns back to me. We stare some more.

"We'd make a good duo," he says, his voice low.

It's my turn to blush, cheeks warm as a sunburn. "I don't know how popular a whistler-banjo act would be."

"Your lips are pretty when you whistle."

I look at Gabe's lips.

He leans across his banjo. I lean to meet him. And we kiss.

*   *   *

Two days later, Jess, Harper and I sit around a low table with the contest entry form. I hold our shiny, perfect CD in one hand, an uncapped permanent marker in the other. "The name of our trio is…"

Jess shakes her head, blank-faced.

"I don't know!" Harper moans. "My brain's too tired from yesterday."

"Slayed With Chops still doesn't do it for you?" I joke.

"No!" Jess and Harper say together.

"Listen to you two, agreeing." Unlike my bandmates, I'm feeling perky.

Two days ago I kissed the cutest banjo player west of anywhere. Yesterday the trio recorded two songs with only minor arguments. And we sounded good. So good I didn't care if Harper sang the lead on both songs.

Today is the deadline to submit our CD. We're in the Tall Grass festival office, which turns out to be in the same building as Crescendo Music, two floors up. Harper knew that, of course.

A man with dreadlocks, red-framed glasses and a Hawaiian shirt watches patiently from a nearby desk. "Don't overthink it, ladies. Your talent is what counts, not your name."

"Someone should have told that to the Goo Goo Dolls," Harper says. "Hey, are those the other entries?" She points to a cardboard box beside his desk. It's stuffed to the brim with white envelopes like the one we're supposed to put our CD and entry form into.

"They are." He smiles and leans over to pat the pile carefully, like it's a sleeping tiger.

Harper and Jess and I exchange grim looks. That pile is what we're up against.

"I don't even want to know how many entries are in there," Harper says.

"One hundred and fourteen," the desk man answers, not helpfully. His phone rings, and before he picks up he adds, "For thirty-five spots."

I do the math. "Add our entry and that's one-fifteen. That means eighty groups who won't get in. Eighty."

Harper looks worried for the first time since Darrell told us about the contest.

"And the deadline's still three hours away. Even more acts could enter," Jess says.

Harper grits her teeth. "Thanks for clarifying that, Miss Hopeless."

"Okay, just call us the Harper Neale Trio." Jess gestures at the CD. "That'll make you more hopeful about our chances."

"Whoa!" Harper puts her hands up. "I know you guys think I'm pushy, but I'm not *that* big of an ego-case. Plus, that's too close to my dad's band's name."

"Argh!" Jess gets up and stalks out to the hallway.

"There she goes again," Harper says.

I hand her the CD and marker. "Hang on a second."

I find Jess looking out a tall window. Her right hand, resting on the window ledge, is wrapped in a wrist guard, sore from the last two days of nonstop guitar.

"You look weird without your guitar," I say, keeping my tone light.

"I feel weird. Gotta take a little break, I guess." She holds up her wrist. "Or a big break, if we don't get into Tall Grass." She gives me a sideways, almost embarrassed look. "I had no idea so many groups would be trying for this."

"Neither did I." We both look out the window. The day's getting darker. Across the street, the lights are on in the Honeycomb Café. "But don't you think we sounded great yesterday?" I'm trying to convince myself as well as Jess.

"All the other acts probably think they sound great too. But eighty of us are wrong."

"Let's not think about that right now."

"We have to." Jess's voice is flat, defeated. "We have to face the fact that we might not be good enough."

I look at her full-on. "You sound like my mom. Only exceptional people succeed, so you might as well give up."

Jess pulls back. "She said that?"

"Close enough. It's what she thought. Is it what you think?"

Jess shrugs.

I'm suddenly angry. "I can't believe you still don't want to try for Tall Grass after all the work we've put into this. There's competition, so we shouldn't bother entering?"

"How good do you really think we are?"

"Fine." I call out, "Harper, we're pulling out."

"Nat! That's not what I said."

Harper charges out of the office. "What's with you two? I was getting the hairy eyeball in there." She doesn't seem to have heard what I said. She makes for the stairs. "He's asked us to go somewhere else until we get this name thing sorted out."

"We don't need a name if we're not entering the contest," I say.

"What?" Harper pivots at the top of the stairs. She jabs a finger toward Jess, her bracelets jangling. "No. You are not pulling this again. You are not wrecking our chance at Tall Grass."

"I know. I'm not. You two need to shut up for a minute."

We do. Jess telling us to shut up is even weirder than Jess without a guitar.

"Sorry. But you got off track with that thing your mom said. Or I got you off track. I don't know." Jess puts her good hand up to her forehead, then lets it drop. "I suck at this. Talking about stuff."

"You said we have to realize we might not be good enough," I prompt her.

"We do."

"Oh, great." Harper flings her hands up.

Jess's eyes stay on mine. "But that doesn't mean I don't want us to enter the contest. I do. More than that, I want us to win one of those spots. It hit me yesterday. The way we worked. The way we sounded. We're good. All three of us." She looks at Harper. "We're good separately and we're good together."

I want to grab my best friend and hug her hard. But that would drive her crazy. I simply say, "We're better together."

Jess points toward the office door. "But you saw all those entries. We might not get in. We have to face that."

"Whoa!" Harper says. "As far as I'm concerned, A, we'll get in—"

"But—"

"Uh-uh!" Harper makes a chopping motion. "And B, if we don't get in...actually, I won't even think about that."

"We can still be a trio," I declare.

The dreadlocks-and-glasses guy leans out of the Tall Grass doorway. "Ladies. There is a café across the street where they would be delighted to serve you all the caffeine you need to fuel your debate. It's called Honeycomb. I suggest you go."

Honeycomb.

I already love the word because of what happened there with Gabe. But something in the way the guy says it—his warm, musical voice—nudges at me.

"Thanks, Robert. We'll do that." Harper waves the white envelope.

"I shall be here, anxiously awaiting the outcome." Robert waves back and disappears.

Honeycomb.

"Robert? I suppose you know him?" Jess asks Harper.

"I do now. I like to get to know people. You should try it."

"I wonder if he's one of the judges."

"If so, I've just improved our chances with my charming ways. You're welcome." Harper heads down the stairs.

"Wait," I say.

Harper stops. "What now?"

"Honeycomb." I sweep my hands out like a magician unveiling a surprise.

Harper and Jess stare, waiting for more.

"Yes, Nat." Harper speaks slowly. "That is where we're going."

"We don't need to go. Honeycomb. Say it."

"Are you having a seizure or something?"

"Honeycomb." Jess breaks into a smile. She gets it. I knew she would.

"Our band name," I say. "Sweet, smooth, natural."

"Perfectly structured," Jess adds.

It dawns on Harper. "Like our harmonies! Honeycomb. It's good."

I take the white envelope and our CD from Harper. "Come on, Honeycomb," I say. "We've got an entry to submit."

Ten

Two weeks later, Harper, Jess, Gabe and I wait in Darrell's office for him to finish a lesson. He said we should check the Tall Grass site together. To emphasize "together" he made us turn off our cell phones and said, "No sneaking a peek before I get back." The results would be posted at noon. The clock on Darrell's desk now reads 12:03. I'm afraid we'll combust from the anticipation.

"We could check on his computer," Harper says, sidling toward Darrell's chair.

"No! Jeez, Harper, have a little patience," Jess says. She leans against the doorframe, hands in her jeans pockets. She looks relaxed, but I've caught her glancing to the hallway about ten

times in the last three minutes. Checking for
Darrell.

Gabe's left leg jiggles against mine like it's
plugged into an overactive circuit board. Harper
watches him but says nothing.

She and Jess found out about Gabe and me
the day of the contest entry. We ended up going
to the Honeycomb Café after all, because Harper
insisted on celebrating our band name. The
tattooed barista gave it away. "Hi again, Songbird!
Where's your boyfriend with the banjo?"

Jess grinned, happy for me. Harper said, "As
long as he doesn't get in the way of the trio."

Now Jess pushes away from the door. "Here
comes Darrell." She perches on the couch arm
beside me, and we exchange anxious smiles.

Darrell swings into the room and drops into
his chair. "Sorry. Long conversation about minor
scales. Thanks for waiting, gang." He takes us in,
then gives a small laugh. "You look like you're
waiting to be sentenced for something. Relax."

"Relax?" Harper says. "This could be the most
important news of my life."

Jess winces, uneasy with Harper's drama.

Darrell sighs and clasps his hands together on the desk. "Listen up. You guys need to remember that what's important in all this is—"

"No!" I can't quite believe that was me, but I also can't stop. "I think what we need is to check the results. Now. Please."

"What, no words of wisdom?" Darrell says, raising an eyebrow.

"No!" we yell.

"Fair enough." Darrell turns his monitor in our direction. We get up and cluster around like it's magnetized. He types. The Tall Grass festival website appears. The mainstage, blue sky, a crowd. I feel a hand grip mine. Harper's.

Darrell scrolls to the Young Performers tab and clicks. Image of a stool, a guitar and a mic on an empty stage. Gabe takes my other hand. Darrell clicks again and a column of names appears. We all strain forward. I skim the list: Hannah Mac... Heavy Lifting...Honeycomb.

"Honeycomb! I knew it. We're in!" Harper squeezes my hand and pulls me into a bouncing, squealing, laughing hug.

We're in, we're in! sings through my brain.

I notice Gabe's hand is gone, though I didn't feel it leave. I turn away from Harper.

Darrell, Jess and Gabe stare at the screen.

Gabe's head drops. Jess puts a hand gently on his shoulder.

Eleven

I can barely look at Gabe when he says, "That's amazing, you guys. I'm totally pumped for you." He's doing a decent impression of cheerful, but his face is pale.

Jess is the first to answer. "I can't believe you're not on that list. It feels wrong."

I don't know what to say. I want to reach out and take Gabe's hand back in mine, but I worry that would be mistaken for pity.

"It sucks," Harper says.

Gabe stares at her, stony-faced. "Thank you, Harper. Yes, it sucks big-time. Listen," he says when he sees Darrell about to talk, "I'm gonna head out. My dad had plans for us to meet up for lunch."

They probably thought they'd have something to celebrate.

Darrell gets up and puts his arm around Gabe's shoulder. "Let me walk you to the door, dude."

As soon as Darrell and Gabe are down the hallway, Harper lets out a yelp of excitement.

Jess spins to face her. "No. You are not doing that right now. No frigging bouncing."

I make sure to stand still.

"Okay, okay," Harper says. "But aren't you even a little psyched? We're performing at Tall Grass!" She grabs me around the waist and gives me a tight shake.

"But Gabe isn't. Can't you, for once, think of someone else?" Jess plunks down on the couch. "Whatever. Never mind."

Harper lets go of me. "'Whatever' is right," she says, making air quotes. "This is hard for Gabe. I get that. I'm sorry about it."

"Are you?"

"Yes, Miss More-Serious-Than-Everyone, I am." Harper fishes her phone out of her bag. "I'm going to go call Grandma Barb. At least she'll be happy about our news."

She bumps into Darrell at the door. He says, "Hey, we've got details to go over. Where are you going?"

Harper aims her answer back into the room. "To talk to someone who gets this stuff. To a real musician." She faces Darrell. "Don't worry, I'll be right back."

She goes, and Darrell turns to me and Jess.

I flop onto the couch, suddenly exhausted. "I guess I should have let you tell us those words of wisdom earlier."

"Nah. Probably wouldn't have helped anyway," Darrell says.

It's the first time I felt like a real musician. Gabe's words from the after-party pop into my head. Now Honeycomb will be at Tall Grass. Like real musicians. And Gabe won't.

Is this how it feels to be a real musician?

* * *

When I get home from Darrell's, Mom is happy, though surprised, to hear that Honeycomb got into the festival. Then I tell her our performance date.

"I think that's when we drive Eric up to hockey camp." She pulls her phone out of her purse. She's all dressed up and ready to go with

Dad and Eric to the end-of-year hockey banquet. She scrolls to the calendar. "Yes. The same day."

She says it as if Tall Grass was organized specifically to conflict with hockey camp.

"I can get a ride with Jess and her mom." I open the fridge and pretend to be deeply interested in what's inside so I can hide my disappointment.

Eric appears, a moth drawn to the fridge light, and reaches past me for a pop.

"The festival's outside the city, isn't it?" Mom asks.

"In Old Plains Park." I close the fridge, empty-handed. "Why?"

"What festival?" Eric cracks open the pop.

"Don't get anything on your white shirt, Eric," Mom says. She leans out to the hallway and yells, "Carl, are you almost ready to go?"

I answer Eric. "The Tall Grass festival. Honeycomb got in."

He wipes at a drop of orange pop on his sleeve. "What's Honeycomb?"

"Nat's trio," Mom answers. "They got into the Young People's competition. That's pretty great."

I'm so surprised she sounds enthusiastic I don't even care that she got the contest name wrong.

"Cool, Nat." Eric gives me a fist bump. Guzzles his pop.

"Thanks. It is kind of a big deal." Amazing. Two family members impressed by my musical accomplishment.

Eric crumples his pop can. "You'll get to hang out with all the potheads who go there."

"Eric!" Why was I stupid enough to think he was impressed?

"What potheads?" Dad comes into the kitchen, wafting aftershave smell.

Eric smirks. "Nat's group is singing at the Smoking Grass Festival."

"What?" Dad swivels in my direction.

"*Tall* Grass *Music* Festival!" I say.

"So...is that good?" Dad asks Mom, his translator.

"It's very good." She herds him and Eric toward the door. "I'll explain in the car. Your son's being ridiculous." She says over her shoulder, "It's lovely news, Nat. We'll see if we can figure something out."

Then they're gone.

"I'm glad you're all so thrilled for me," I say into the silence.

*   *   *

Alone in the basement, I take advantage of the empty house to practice singing scales at the piano. I hate doing it when Eric's on the game player, or when Mom or Dad comes down for laundry.

My phone vibrates beside me on the bench. Finally. A text from Gabe. I've texted him about ten times since he left Darrell's office earlier.

Thnx for txts. I'm fine. Don't need to call me. U shld prob focus on T Grass. Good luck.

I scroll back to see if I somehow missed an earlier message. Nothing. I let the phone drop back onto the bench and close the lid over the piano keyboard.

Twelve

A week later the trio is back at the Tall Grass office to meet our new mentor.

Robert is behind the desk, sporting green glasses today and an ivory tunic. "Welcome back, Loud Ladies of the Hallway. All has worked out, I see."

"It has," Harper says, beaming.

Except it hasn't. I haven't heard from Gabe since he sent that single text. Plus Jess is pissed off at the idea of a new mentor.

When Darrell reminded us about the mentor the day the results were announced, Jess complained, "I don't want to work with someone new. This ridiculous contest makes everything so complicated."

Darrell said, "Try to embrace the opportunity."

Jess hasn't exactly embraced it, but she's here. I'm determined to embrace everything about Tall Grass. It's the best thing in my life right now.

"Honeycomb, Honeycomb," Robert says, flipping through papers. "Ah, you are to work with Ingrid Leo." He makes it sound like we are being introduced to royalty. "An exceptional musician. An exceptional teacher."

"See, Jess? This'll be good for us," I say.

"More than good," Robert says. "Transforming."

"Wow," says Harper. "That's quite the endorsement."

"Ingrid is my wife. Quite terrifying." Robert winks. "She's down the hall, the orange door on the left. You have precisely one hour. You've brought your music, I trust?"

"Of course," Harper answers for us.

When we arrive at the orange door, two guys come out. They're dressed all in black from their wool hats to their boots, and one carries a coffin-shaped guitar case. As they pass us, one says, "That was harsh, bro. I feel sorta dizzy."

The other replies, "Same here. But not, like, in a good way."

"Wonderful," Jess mumbles.

Harper leads Jess and me into the room and puts on her sparkly voice. "Hello? It's Honeycomb."

A tiny, porcelain-skinned woman stands barefoot in the middle of the room. She has spiky blond hair and wears a boxy, origami-like shirt over black tights.

I've seen her before. She was the impatient customer at Crescendo Music. The one with all the books. The one Bushy-Beard was afraid of.

"Well, that last group was unprepared." A voice strong as a tuba coming out of the body of a doll. "Let's see how you three fare."

* * *

Twenty minutes into our session, Ingrid Leo plants one of her surprisingly large hands on my stomach. "Breathe in so my hand is forced outward," she commands.

I try.

A dismissive grunt. "Again. Mean it this time."

Mean my breath? I try again.

Ingrid withdraws her hand. My breath is disappointing to her. She didn't pay all this attention to Harper's breathing. "Let me show you." She takes one of my hands and flattens it on her crisp shirt, over her stomach. I do my best to pretend I'm totally relaxed about this. One of her hair spikes almost stabs me in the eye.

"Picture the breath going behind the lungs, behind and under." Ingrid takes a breath, and I feel my hand being pushed away. "Emotion lives in our solar plexus, so that's where breath needs to go. To where our emotion lives."

My hand vibrates from the force of her voice. "Wow."

"You see?" Ingrid smiles at me. "Every note—every emotion—needs to be supported by enough breath. It takes lifelong practice."

Jess, sitting beside Harper on the floor, leans back on her hands. "I'm all for lifelong practice, but the festival's in July. We've been warming up for half an hour. Are we going to get to the actual songs today?"

"Jess!" Harper stands up, as if Jess is suddenly contagious.

"Come over here, Jess." Ingrid's voice is somehow creamy and steely at the same time. "Harper, you too."

She makes us face each other, about three feet apart. "The chorus in 'Blue Skywriting,' it changes throughout the song, doesn't it?"

"Well, the lyrics stay the same," Harper says. She hurries over to her bag to get the music, which she hands to Ingrid.

Jess shakes her head, dismissive. "But the emotion behind the chorus can change, depending on what's happened in the verse before it. I already know that."

"Maybe you know that here"—Ingrid reaches up and taps Jess's head—"but not here"—she taps her stomach. "I could hear that on your CD."

We take that in. Ingrid must have been one of the judges if she heard our CD.

"Sing the bridge and the final chorus."

Starting at the bridge means starting with Harper on melody. Better her than me.

"I need my guitar," says Jess.

"Let's focus on the voice for now. And you girls are good enough to find the notes without help," Ingrid says, cutting off what was likely Jess's next protest. "Go ahead."

There's no escape. Harper sings the bridge, Jess and I come in on the proper lines of the chorus, Harper finishes on the last *swept me away.*

"Perfectly adequate," Ingrid says. "Now, take each other's hands and close your eyes."

Jess snorts. Even Harper looks skeptical.

Ingrid says, "Yes, I'm sure this all feels too kumbaya for words. Do it anyway."

We join hands. I'm surprised at how cold Harper's are. Cold and slightly shaky. Could she be nervous? Jess's grip is loose, which makes me hold tighter. I close my eyes. I have to trust that Jess and Harper do too.

"Your closed eyes will help you listen to each other. Harmony takes listening. It will also help you concentrate on your breathing." Ingrid's voice is surprisingly gentle. "Breathe right down to the very bottom of your belly. Take a few breaths now, before you begin."

We do. It's strange at first, then calming, hearing nothing but Jess's and Harper's breathing so close by. We have to count on each other.

Ingrid says, "Start with all of you singing the bridge this time."

Harper hums the opening note for us and we begin: "*But the clouds, you brought them on /*

*and the words you wrote, now they are gone /
you've left me here, no sign of dawn..."*

Jess sings: "*With your blue skywriting...*"

Jess and I sing: "*Bright blue skywriting...*"

Harper joins us: "*Blue skywriting...*"

Then she finishes: "*Swept me away.*"

"Better. Now, open your eyes. Sing again,"
Ingrid says, wasting no time. "Full, supportive
breaths."

As soon as we hit *you've left me here, no sign
of dawn*, Jess's eyes rim with tears. She blinks
hard and takes a deep breath for the next two
lines. Her voice comes out so rich that Harper's
high melody sounds glassy over it, almost in
danger of cracking. At the end, Harper's solo line,
swept me away, sounds truly alone. The way the
songwriter means it to.

I get it.

Jess pulls away and gives her eyes a quick
swipe.

Ingrid hands the music back to Harper, who
takes it without a word. "Think of what we can
do when we get to the full songs, Jess," Ingrid
says lightly. "See you girls next week."

* * *

Jess powers down the stairs ahead of us.

Not that Harper notices. "That was amazing. Ingrid is intense! I'm already more aware of my voice."

Harper's so loud everybody in the building is probably aware of her voice. "I never knew how hard it was to breathe properly," I say as we follow Jess outside.

"It's not that hard, Nat." Jess's voice is cool. The wind blows her dark hair across her face.

"Okay, maybe not hard." I tuck my own hair behind my ears. "But I know you felt the difference when we—"

"The voice is an instrument, you know, Jess," Harper interrupts. "It takes as much practice as a guitar."

"Oh yeah? How much guitar do you play?" Jess heads toward the bus stop.

Harper steps in front of her. "I play piano, my mom plays piano, my dad plays guitar and about five other instruments, Grandma Barb plays guitar and piano. I'm surrounded by instruments."

Jess does two slow claps. "Bravo. You're a frigging musical dynasty."

"And you're a frigging pain in the butt."

"Stop it!" I get between them. "We had a good session with Ingrid. At least, I thought it was good. We get to play at Tall Grass. Why do we have to fight about what an instrument is?"

Jess looks at me as if I'm clueless. "Because, Nat, we wasted an hour making zombie noises and *feeling* things when we should be working on our harmonies and making sure the guitar is balanced with the vocals."

"So you don't think there need to be feelings in a song?" I hold her gaze.

"For the audience." Jess doesn't blink. "When the notes are right, the feelings take care of themselves. A musician's job is to get the notes right." She crosses her arms. "You were flat in the chorus."

There's a weird pause in the wind. I feel off balance.

"Nice, Jess. Really nice," Harper says.

Jess goes on. "That's the sort of stuff we need to work on. Not Ingrid's stupid exercises."

I put up my hands. "Okay, Jess, I get it. Ingrid bugs you. Harper bugs you. I bug you. Fine." I shove my hands in my pockets and back away. "You know what? I'm going to head over to the café. If anyone else needs a great big hot chocolate right about now, they're welcome to join me."

"I'm coming," Harper says.

"Great."

The wind blows a dirty coffee cup into my path, and I kick it aside.

Thirteen

arper picks the table by the window, the same one Gabe and I sat at our first time here. I wish I could talk to him right now. I sit, still shaky from whatever it was that just happened between me and Jess.

Harper raises her cup. "Here's to Nat."

"Okay." I raise my cup and Harper clinks it. "Why, exactly?"

"For not taking crap from Jess." Harper adjusts her windswept curls. "Ingrid puts her in her place and she takes it out on you—'you were flat.'"

"Maybe I was."

"You definitely were not. Trust me, I'd tell you if you were." She warms her hands on her cup.

"Wait. Did Harper Neale just compliment me on my singing?"

"Ha-ha," she says, sarcastic.

I take that as a yes. I'll take anything I can get to feel better about my place in the trio.

"You know what, Nat? Jess holds you back."

I stop basking in the glow of Harper's semi-praise. "I don't know about that."

She sighs. "You're going to say, 'Jess and I are BFFs. Why would she hold me back?'"

"I would *not* say BFFs."

Harper ignores my comment. "But if you honestly felt she wasn't holding you back, you wouldn't have stood up to her. That was fierce, Nat."

I shift in my chair, uncomfortable. "Thank you, Dr. Neale. What do I owe you for this session?"

Harper sits back and sips her hot chocolate. "You know I'm right."

"But I'm doing what I want to be doing—prepping for Tall Grass, improving my singing."

"You're doing it, but are you feeling it?"

I give a little laugh. "Feelings again." I glance out the window. A woman walks by, clutching her coat closed against the wind.

"Are you excited about Honeycomb? About Tall Grass?"

"Of course!" I turn back to Harper.

Her voice goes quiet. "So why don't you show it?"

"I do." Harper's expression doesn't change. "Don't I?"

"You try. But"—she holds up her fingers as she makes her points—"Darrell says we should try out for Tall Grass. You get excited; Jess walks out. We get into Tall Grass. You get excited; Jess tells you to stop. We make a breakthrough during a session with Ingrid. You get excited; Jess shoots you down."

Harper's words sit there like cards snapped down on the table. She takes a last slow sip of her hot chocolate.

"Jess feels things differently than I do."

Harper jabs a finger onto the table. "That doesn't mean she should tell you how to feel."

Jess does get annoyed when I'm too enthusiastic. But she's also had my back from the time we were kids. Until lately.

"That's it, let my wisdom sink in. 'Cause now I totally need to pee." Harper laughs and stands up. "Be right back."

The baristo comes by, picks up Harper's cup and points to my half-empty one. "You done with this?"

I nod. "It was a bit too much for me." I glance out the window.

And see Gabe walking into Crescendo Music.

"Tell my friend 'sorry, but something came up.'" I'm out the door before the guy can answer.

*   *   *

Gabe's back is to me, his head bent as he flips through a book. He's wearing the same plaid shirt he had on at Harper's after-party I have to stop myself from reaching out to touch it. "Hey. Good book?"

He turns. His face shuts down so fast I'm tempted to bolt. But I keep smiling.

Gabe doesn't smile back. "I don't know. I haven't read it yet."

"Right." I swallow. "I was across the street and saw you and...I wanted to say hi. See how you're doing."

"I'm fine. Still banjoing away." He looks past me. "You and your bandmates still arguing?" He says "bandmates" as if he's forgotten their names.

I wish I hadn't decided to follow him in here. "No." It's not a total lie. Harper seems to be suddenly on my side.

"Well, good luck keeping that up." Now he smiles.

"Uh, thanks."

"At least as a solo act I'm free of that crap."

"I guess that's a good way to look at it," I say, missing the guy who talked about people being happy together at Tall Grass.

His cheeks flush. He looks down at the book and hefts it. "Think I'll get this. See you."

He starts to walk away and I say, "Gabe?"

He turns.

"I'm not the reason you didn't get into Tall Grass."

Gabe bites his lip. Looks away. Looks back. I can barely hear him when he says, "I know."

I watch him until he's at the counter, talking with Bushy-Beard. I can't leave the store without going past him. I go to the other side of the book rack, crouch down and pull a random book off the lowest shelf. I try not to cry.

*   *   *

A week later, Harper and I stop outside the closed orange door. I was sure Jess would be here already, but she's not.

"You're at school with her all week," Harper whispers angrily. "You're basically joined at the hip but she doesn't tell you she's going to be late?"

Jess and I haven't spoken this week. I whisper back, "When I got to her place her mom said she had left an hour earlier. Maybe she had stuff to do and she'll be here any minute."

"Any minute will be too late."

The orange door swings open. Harper grabs my hand like we're in a horror movie.

"Are you unfamiliar with how doorknobs work?" Ingrid is barefoot and in tights again, but with a droopy sweater that looks like it's knitted out of spider webs and poodle hair.

Harper ducks into the room ahead of me. Ingrid must be the first person who's ever intimidated her.

"Sorry Jess isn't here yet," I say, figuring it's best to get the bad news out quickly.

"Jess won't be here." Ingrid turns her back and closes the door with a firm click. "She phoned here and told Robert she wasn't well."

"Huh." Harper looks at me.

But all I have are questions. Jess went out, so she can't be sick. So where did she go? And why didn't she tell me?

Ingrid strides over to the window and presses a button on a timer that's perched on the windowsill. Green digital numbers begin to count down our hour. She puts her hands on her hips. "Today we are going to work at your *passaggio*. Do you know that term?"

"It sounds familiar." Harper squints, trying to squeeze the answer out of her head. I can't even pretend to know what it means.

Ingrid prowls around the room. "The term is Italian, obviously, and refers to the place in your register where the chest voice shifts into the head voice."

"Oh! The vocal break," Harper says.

Ingrid purses her lips. "'Break' is the wrong term. The shift must be smooth, continuous. A passage. Passaggio."

Harper nods. It's odd to see her look happy while being told she's wrong about something musical.

"Nat, you need to work on this more than Harper does," Ingrid says.

That perks Harper up even more.

We do a short vocal warm-up. Then Ingrid orders me to the middle of the room. "Sing the first verse of 'Blue Skywriting' for me."

"That's actually my part of the song," Harper says.

But Ingrid waves that aside. "You should all know every part of the song."

So I sing the verse. I feel my chest tense when I have to hit the higher notes. Of course, the tell-tale crack happens.

"There." Ingrid pounces.

"When I'm more relaxed I can—"

Ingrid holds up a hand. "I know. I'm not punishing you—I'm helping you. Now do me a favor. Repeat after me." She sings,

"Boo-boo-boo-boo-boo," three notes up, two down.

I do the same. We go up through a few octaves this way.

"Nice and smooth. That's why I start with narrow vowels. This gets more difficult with open vowels." She sings the line "*Said you had to astound me*," putting a break in her voice on "had" and "astound."

"I never thought of the vowel sounds as being the hard part. I thought it was the notes." Now that I seem to have done something right, I don't mind if I say something stupid.

"It's both, of course. But the back of the throat has to make a different shape for the different vowel sounds. The *ah* requires a higher larynx, and the *ooh* a lower one. But enough mechanics." Ingrid glances at the timer. "Harper, come join us."

Harper stands beside me.

"We'll do what we did with *boo*, but using *bah*. You'll both be my little sheep."

I can imagine what Jess would say to that.

Ingrid leads us through scales of *bah*, interrupting with "Support it with your breath" or "Don't think steps, think passage." She moves the entire time, while Harper and I stand in the center of the room. Hardworking sheep.

I love it. My voice gets stronger and freer with every breath.

Ingrid stops in front of me. "Now. Sing your line again."

I breathe in. "*Said you had to astound me.*" No cracks.

Ingrid claps. "You see? Lovely. Keep working on this, girls. Every day. Always work. To astound your audience." She winks at me.

Harper and I high-five each other. We're a team. Without Jess.

*   *   *

Alone on the bus going home, I get a text from Gabe. Was jerk when I saw u. Actually hope practices for TGrass going good.

I feel a smile take over my face, then look around at the other passengers, as if one of them will tell me not to let Gabe off so easily. I wait until the end of my ride before I answer, You were. They are.

He immediately answers, :-)

I put my phone away, content to leave it at that for now.

Fourteen

When I get to the Tall Grass office the following Saturday, Robert says, "Your bandmates are out in the square today."

"We're having our session there? Like, outdoors out?"

"Precisely outdoors out."

I hurry over. I'm determined to be completely professional today. I've been doing my breathing and passaggio exercises all week. And avoiding Jess. That hasn't been difficult. I think she's avoiding me too. Neither of us called the other about getting here today. Whatever. I'm focused on music.

I reach the square and see Ingrid at the far end. She's wearing a multicolored poncho and shooing three sullen smokers away from the bandshell. Jess sits on a bench, absorbed in her usual guitar tuning. Harper stands away from both of them, sipping from a water bottle. When she spots me, she hurries over and grabs my arm.

"Have you talked to Jess lately?" She speaks from the side of her mouth, like she's afraid Jess can lip-read.

"Harper, I want to concentrate on our rehearsal. I don't want to talk about Jess holding me back or whatever."

"Oh yeah? Would you rather talk about Jess and Gabe coming out of Darrell's together?"

I pull my arm away. "What?"

"I was on my way here. My bus goes past DBML. The two of them stroll out, laughing." Harper points her water bottle at Jess. "I bet that's why Jess missed last week with Ingrid. It's why she didn't tell you. Jess wasn't sick. She's been busy with Gabe."

Ingrid sees us. "Ah, now we are complete. Let's get started."

"You need to talk to her," Harper says and jogs to the stage.

Jess ambles over to me. "I think rehearsing outside is a fantastic idea," she says. "Better than that stuffy room over at the Tall Grass office."

"Did Ingrid give you a hard time about missing last week?" It's as close as I can get to asking her about being with Gabe at Darrell's.

"Nope." Jess steps up onto the stage, next to Harper. "I just wasn't up for it last week. I'm feeling better now."

"Gee, I wonder why?" says Harper.

Jess either doesn't hear or chooses to ignore her.

Gabe texted me just after the session with Ingrid. Was he with Jess then? Was that why he asked how our practices were going?

Ingrid throws me an impatient look. The music, I remind myself, joining Harper and Jess. Focus on the music.

*   *   *

Ingrid stands about forty feet away from the bandshell. "Let me hear that again. I know you'll have mics at Tall Grass, but you still need to project more. Wind direction can toss your voices around, so it's good to be prepared."

A delivery truck reverses into a loading dock nearby, *beep-beeping* the whole time. A pack of yelling kids chase each other over the grass in front of the stage. Their moms gab on a bench. Not exactly the treed setting and attentive audience we hope to have at Tall Grass.

"One sec?" I call to Ingrid and grab one of the bottles of water she brought for us. "I'm a little thirsty."

"You okay?" Jess asks.

I recap the water, avoiding her eyes. "Yep. Let's go."

We try "I've Got This Friend" again. Harper's got the melody, of course. I'm having trouble hearing her well enough to know if my harmonies are in key. But every time I inch closer to her, she inches closer to the front of the stage. Jess, used to singing over her own guitar playing, seems unworried.

Ingrid waves her hands. "Harper and Nat, back up so you're still close to Jess. Stay under the roofline. When you're too far forward, your voices diffuse into the air."

Harper takes three giant steps back. "Stop crowding me, Nat. My arms move when I sing. I don't want to bash you."

"It's not punk music, Harper," Jess says. "You don't have to thrash around. Nat needs to be close to hear you."

A piercing whistle shocks us all into silence. Even the running kids stop in their tracks. Ingrid removes her fingers from her mouth. "You're wasting time, girls. From the top again."

Jess counts us in. I can hear Harper better, but I feel stiff standing still, trying not to crowd her. Looking across to Jess, her face serene as she plays and sings, I feel a stab of jealousy. Has Darrell been telling her what a superior musician she is compared to Harper and me? Has Gabe watched her sing and told her how pretty her lips are?

"I can't hear you again, Nat." Ingrid's voice jolts. She's stepped onstage without me noticing. "Your breathing is too shallow. That's bad enough indoors, but outdoors you're sunk."

"Right. I know."

Ingrid tucks in between Harper and me and puts her hands on my back and stomach. Not this again. "Start at the chorus. All of you. Nat, get that breath of yours to move my hands, the way I showed you in our first session."

A little girl has wandered over to the band-shell. She stares up at me, sucking thoughtfully on her juice-box straw.

I take a deep breath. We start the chorus. Ingrid's hands feel heavy. I work to move them. I mess up a word and Harper stink-eyes me over Ingrid's head. I wish more than anything that Ingrid would take her hands away. I breathe. The little girl pops the straw out of her mouth and tries to sing along. My voice cracks.

"Passaggio!" Ingrid says.

I breathe. We move into the next verse. Two trucks rumble by, one honking. Jess leans in closer with her guitar, bobs her head as if to say, "You're off the beat." I breathe. Ingrid takes her hands away but comes around in front and stares at me, her pale eyebrows furrowed. The little girl yells, "I can't see." My voice cracks again.

"Stop." Ingrid puts her hands on her head, smushing down her spikes.

"Well, that sucked," Harper says not so quietly.

"You're pushing," Ingrid says. "You're going to hurt your voice if you keep that up."

"Sorry. There's too much going on." My throat feels scratchy.

The little girl's mom takes her hand, saying, "Leave the singers alone, Maya."

"They're not singers," Maya corrects her. She has no problem projecting. "They're only pretending."

She's right. At least about me.

"There'll be a lot going on at the festival too." Ingrid studies me. She's the doctor, I'm the problem patient. "Have you been to Tall Grass?"

"Oh, please," Jess mumbles.

I swear I can feel Harper's smugness wafting off her like a smell. Anger spills over inside me. "No, I have not been to Tall Grass. Or any outdoor music festival. I have not taken singing lessons all my life. I don't play an instrument. I can barely sight-read music. I'm a school choir dropout, an amateur. I shouldn't be here. I shouldn't be at the Tall Grass festival."

Ingrid's expression hasn't changed. "You're not helping your voice with an outburst like that."

"I quit," I say. "I quit Honeycomb." I run off the stage and keep running. Someone calls my name, but I can't tell if it's Harper or Jess. Not that either of them needs me.

Fifteen

An hour later, I'm all cried out. I lie on my bed, staring at the ceiling. *I quit Honeycomb* repeats in my head. Beside me, my phone is quiet. I had half expected a frantic Come back text from Harper. Nothing.

There's a knock at my door.

"I told you, Mom." My voice rasps. I clear my throat. "It was just a lousy rehearsal. I'm fine."

I haven't told her yet that I've quit the group. She'll probably be relieved.

My door opens.

I drop my arm over my eyes. "Mom, I said—"

"You're right. It was a lousy rehearsal," Jess says.

I move my arm. "Go away."

She leans against the doorframe. "I thought I was the expert at walking away from stuff I hate, but you showed me. Impressive."

"Did you come here to gloat?"

"No." She closes the door behind her. "I came to make sure you're okay."

"I'm fine," I say, though the pile of tissues beside the bed probably gives me away. I sit up. "You can still gloat. Because you were right. This whole Tall Grass contest was a stupid idea. Especially for me. Today's rehearsal proved it." Something catches in my chest. I grit my teeth, hold back the tears. "But you knew all along. Sorry I dragged you through all this."

Jess sits on the bed. "You dragged me through to being a better musician."

"Great. You can go off and be a better musician without me."

"To perform with only Harper? As if that would work." Jess smiles at me.

Looking at her, so straightforward, so steady, I can see exactly why Gabe would fall for her.

"Or with Gabe."

"Gabe?"

"Don't play dumb." My heart races. "Harper told me she saw you and Gabe coming out of Darrell's today. Together. She figures that's why you missed our session with Ingrid and didn't tell me. I figure that's why you've barely talked to me lately. Because you're seeing Gabe."

Jess tilts her head. "Seeing Gabe? Like, going out with him?"

I almost yell, "Yes, like going out with him."

"Argh. Harper and her drama." She gets off the bed. "What sort of a friend does she think I am?"

"I don't know. The sort who doesn't tell me things."

Jess holds her hands out as if to steady herself. "There was nothing to tell. I'm not seeing Gabe. We both wanted help, and Darrell squeezed me in to some of Gabe's lessons. Gabe was nice enough to let that happen. One of those times was when Honeycomb was supposed to meet with Ingrid. I had to choose. I chose Darrell. Good thing, 'cause I'm much better at the songs, thanks to him."

"Why didn't you tell me all that?"

Jess deflates. "It sounds stupid now."

I wait, arms crossed.

"I was embarrassed." Jess slides down to the floor, her back against the bed. "I've never been embarrassed about music before, but that session with Ingrid—the breathing, the emotions, the solar plexus stuff it felt too...messy. Not musical. It scared me."

"I've never seen you scared."

She pushes back her hair. "Well, that's what it looks like. Not pretty."

I remember how powerful our voices sounded, how the song made sense to me. "I loved that exercise," I admit.

Jess rests her head back onto the bed. "I could tell. You and Harper. That bugged me. How could you two get something so easily and I couldn't? I knew I needed Darrell's help after that session, when you blew up at me. I thought, If Nat's mad, I need to do something."

"It doesn't matter anymore," I say. "I've quit. You can quit. Harper can do what she wants. We don't have to deal with her or Ingrid."

"Or Honeycomb?"

I nod.

"After all the work we've done?"

I say what Harper said in our first meeting at Darrell's. "Just because you worked hard on something doesn't mean it's the right thing to do."

Jess gets up and sits on the bed. "Remember in March, in my bedroom? You told me you wanted to try to be a real musician."

"I was deluded."

"You weren't. Because now you *are* a real musician. Over the past couple of months, you've become one." Jess smiles, waiting for a response.

"Not today I wasn't."

She waves that off. "Every musician has bad rehearsals sometimes. It's part of the process. The way Grandma Barb said arguments are part of the process."

"We perfected that part of the process."

"It's Harper's specialty."

"You're pretty good at it too."

Jess opens her mouth, fake-shocked.

I can't help smiling.

"The trio only survived all those arguments because of you. You're what held us together." She nudges my foot with hers.

"That's me being nice. That's not me being musical."

"Now look who's arguing. Being able to keep things together—people, music—that takes a stronger sense of harmony than Harper or I will ever have."

Could that be true?

"Plus you're an awesome singer." Jess is matter-of-fact. "Face it. You're a musician. Honeycomb can't exist without you. You aren't allowed to quit. I don't think you want to."

"You'd actually still work with Harper?"

"I will if you will."

The words spark a memory of Jess and me saying that to each other when we were little and getting up the nerve to join the school choir.

Before I can answer Jess, my phone buzzes. I pick it up. "Ha. Guess who." I say to her.

"Tell her the good news."

"I haven't said yes yet."

Jess gives me a friendly push. "Just answer the phone."

"Hey, Harper—"

"Thanks for killing the trio." Her voice is thick.

"No, everything's okay. Jess is here. I changed my mind about Honeycomb," I say.

"Too late," Harper says. "I looked at the Tall Grass website. Honeycomb's not on the Young Performers list anymore. You wrecked everything."

My heart drops.

Jess looks at me, questioning.

"Meet me and Jess outside the Tall Grass office," I say. "We're on our way."

* * *

Jess and I round the corner and see Harper in a spotlight of late-afternoon sun, waiting in front of the Tall Grass building. She leans against the wall, head down, and kicks at the bricks with the heel of her boot.

"She's going to knock the place down," Jess says.

I'm more worried she's going to knock us down. "Harper," I call.

She lifts her head as we approach. "Thanks for quitting Honeycomb and stranding me."

"I know you're probably angry, but—"

"Probably?" Harper pushes away from the wall. "We get a chance to sing at Tall Grass. Something any band would kill for. But you throw it away. This was my dream! So yeah, I'm angry. Because now I realize I was an idiot to include you two." She starts to cry, and her hands fly up to her face.

Jess and I are shocked into silence. On the way over, we'd planned how we'd deal with an annoyed Harper, how we'd let her vent a bit before going into the Tall Grass office to sort everything out. We hadn't planned on a defeated Harper.

She wipes at her eyes, stares at us and lets out a harsh laugh. "Why did I even bother to meet you here? Forget it." She straightens her shoulders and turns to leave. A pigeon ruffles and scoots out of her way.

"Wait." I grab Harper's hand. When she looks at it, angry, I reach out and take her other hand, more gently. "You came because you've always believed in the trio. You saw what we could do before Jess or I did. And you're still ready to fight for it."

Harper's eyes soften for a second. Then she pulls her hands away. "There's nothing to fight for. Honeycomb doesn't exist. You quit." Then she points at Jess. "You abandoned us."

"Hey, I went to get guitar help from Darrell so I could be *better* for Honeycomb. I wasn't abandoning anything. And I sure wasn't 'seeing' Gabe. How was telling Nat that supposed to help the trio?"

"It's not like you were telling her what you were really doing. I was trying to be her friend."

"By upsetting her so much she blew a rehearsal with Ingrid?"

For the hundredth time I come between Harper and Jess. "That. Doesn't. Matter." I pull the two of them over to a nearby bench and make them sit down. "I want to be in Honeycomb. Jess wants to be in Honeycomb. Harper, do you?"

She looks at me like I've asked the stupidest question. "Of course I do. I don't care how much you guys drive me crazy, we sound brilliant together." She pauses, then laughs and shakes her head. "It's true. Weird. Our voices get along even when we can't."

"It's like the music knows something we don't," I say.

"Music knows everything." Harper spreads her hands wide, then rests them on her lap.

Jess leans back, her elbows on the top of the bench. "Yep."

Jess and Harper can't see it, but they both wear the same peaceful expression. The last time I saw that was when we were singing at the March-break showcase.

I sit down beside Jess. "So Honeycomb still exists."

Harper turns to me. "Not on the Tall Grass website."

"Let's go take care of that," I say.

* * *

Robert looks ambushed when Jess, Harper and I charge into the office. "Ladies. What's this?"

Harper slaps her hands down on his desk. "We need to see Ingrid."

"She doesn't live here, you know. Although it feels that way lately." Robert sighs. "It happens that she is in rehearsal with Feathered Hair. A very *restrained* duo."

"Unlike us, you mean?" Jess says.

We hear a familiar voice projecting down the hall. "Keep yawning. Your jaws are too tense.

Yawning helps." Ingrid, fiddling with her timer, appears. "Robert, do you have batteries? Oh!" She notices the three of us.

Robert adjusts his red glasses. "I told the ladies you were busy in rehearsal."

"You owe us an explanation," Harper says.

"So I got your attention, did I?" Ingrid smiles without looking friendly.

Harper's voice goes dark. "Taking Honeycomb off the Young Performers list was your way of getting our attention?"

I hear Robert's desk drawer bang shut.

"Well, didn't you quit?" Ingrid asks.

"No!" I say. "I mean, I know I *said* that, but I was upset and frustrated and..."

Ingrid takes the batteries from Robert. "I'm too busy with the other groups to waste energy on one that isn't committed."

"How many times do we have to tell people?" Harper says, her voice frantic. "We *are* committed."

Ingrid casually jiggles the batteries in her hand, like they're dice. "To missing our sessions? Running out on rehearsals? Declaring you quit?"

"Of course not," Jess says.

"I wanted you to think of the consequences of those behaviors." Ingrid pops the new batteries into her timer. "You all have excellent voices. But perhaps you're just not ready for Tall Grass."

"I can't believe this is happening." Harper speaks barely above a whisper. Her eyes are welling up again. That makes my own eyes prickle with tears.

Ingrid lifts her chin, considers Harper more closely. "I might be willing to give you girls one more chance. Perhaps next Saturday, if you're truly able to commit."

The way she makes it sound like she's doing us a huge favor sticks in my throat. I feel like I should say something, but before I can think of what, Harper nods frantically and says, "Yes. I promise you won't be—"

"Um, Ingrid?" A tall skinny girl pokes her head around the corner into the office. She has—no surprise—feathered hair. "I think we're all yawned out."

"Really?" Jess says, hands on her hips. "Have you tried closing your eyes? Holding hands? Closing your eyes, holding hands and yawning?

Or maybe try singing. That'll loosen your jaws."

Ingrid's head swivels in Jess's direction. So does Robert's. The girl from Feathered Hair backs out of the room.

"Jess, are you crazy?" Harper cries.

And in that frozen moment, I get it. This is how we work. Jess annoyed and blunt, Harper passionate and self-centered, me anxious to keep the peace. But each time they argued, we all worked harder. And that work has created Honeycomb. We don't need Ingrid or Darrell to tell us if we're ready for Tall Grass. We just need to do it. I don't need to keep quiet anymore. I need to use my voice.

Ingrid stalks toward the office door.

I call, "Is there a rule that says we have to work with a mentor in order to be eligible to perform at Tall Grass?"

That stops her. Turning, she pins Robert to the spot. "You're the expert, darling. Is there?"

He shifts from foot to foot. "It is, of course, absolutely recommended. It is a huge benefit for the young musicians who get into Tall Grass..." His rich voice fades to nothing when he looks at the three of us.

"But?" Ingrid prompts.

"No. They do not have to work with a mentor in order to perform." He sits back down.

I don't even try to hold back my smile. "Thank you for all your help, Ingrid. We've learned so much. I know I have for sure. But Honeycomb won't be working with you anymore." Over her shoulder, I see Jess's eyes go wide. Harper makes a little squealing noise. "If that's okay with you guys?"

"Yes!" They say it in perfect unison.

"Well," Ingrid says, short on words for once. "Good luck."

She leaves us for Feathered Hair. I don't envy them for a minute.

"That was stellar, Nat." Jess surprises me by putting her arm around my shoulder and squeezing me close. "Well said."

"Thanks." From here on it's just the three of us, working in argumentative harmony. "Let's get out of here."

"Hang on." Harper turns to Robert, who looks a bit stunned by what's happened. "Can you pull up the website? Honeycomb needs to be back on that list."

"Happily, ladies, happily."

As he types, Jess says, "Great shirt, by the way."

Robert pulls his T-shirt tight. It reads *Words fail. Music speaks.* He chuckles. "You know, my wife hates it."

For once, my words didn't fail. Now our music won't either. Not if I can help it.

Sixteen

The night before the Tall Grass festival, I'm singing scales at the piano in the basement when my phone buzzes. Gabe. Darrell offering to bring me to TG 2morrow 2 see Honeycomb? But ok if u say no. :-)

I smile to myself and text back, call me right now.

I hold the phone and remember the terrible moment in Darrell's office when Gabe realized he didn't get into Tall Grass. How hard he had to work to look like it was okay. How I couldn't come up with anything to say to him.

My cell rings. I take a breath. "Hey."

"Hey. So, uh. It's been...I was such a..."

"How are you?"

Gabe takes a breath too. "I'm okay. Yeah. Good, actually."

"How's your banjo?"

He laughs. "Banjo's good. It says hi and, uh, it misses you."

I hear a strum of the banjo through the phone. I play a few notes on the piano in answer. "It'd be great if you come to Tall Grass tomorrow, Gabe."

"It would? Sweet! I'll tell Darrell. We're looking forward to it."

"Me too. Listen, I have to go. Gotta practice."

"Right. Okay. So. See you tomorrow?"

"See you."

After that, singing scales feels like singing the sweetest song ever written.

* * *

Jess, Harper and I stand in the hot, stuffy shade of the performers' tent at Tall Grass. Other musicians mill about in varying states of nerves. Harper's confession when she arrived a minute ago has put me into the super-nervous category. I take hold of her shoulders. "A sore throat? How could you have a sore throat?"

"From staying up late, I guess. My mom and dad got into town last night so they could see the show." She gestures past the tent, in the direction of the noisy crowd. "They're out there in the audience with Grandma Barb. I'm so excited! I'll be okay, Nat."

"You better be." I try to sound bossy and upbeat.

"I've had some Thayers throat lozenges—my mom says singers swear by them. I'm good to go." Her voice cracks, and her hand goes up to her neck.

"Stop talking," Jess commands. "You've got a water bottle? Don't answer out loud."

Harper nods and holds one up.

"Good," Jess says. "No sore throat's gonna stop us now that we've made it here."

We take in our surroundings. There's a scattering of plastic chairs, though the only person sitting is a girl with a huge Afro, tuning her cello. Everyone else is more into pacing and hugging. The two guys in black who had their sessions with Ingrid before us are huddled in a corner, still in wool hats and heavy boots despite the July heat. A banner hanging from one wall of the tent, says, *Welcome, Tall Grass Young Performers!*

I take some deep, calming breaths, the way Ingrid showed us. The air smells of sun-warmed canvas, vinegar from a nearby abandoned plate of fries, and sunscreen. I decide it's a fantastic combination.

"So." I grab Jess's and Harper's hands. "This is a little different than the backstage of that church in March."

Harper grins.

"This is the real deal," Jess says.

While that makes me nervous, I have faith in Honeycomb. This last month, working on our own in Grandma Barb's sunny attic, we learned to help—and to trust—each other. The arguments don't frighten me anymore. Part of the process.

A woman with a headset and a yellow Tall Grass Volunteer shirt approaches us. "You're up next, Honeycomb. All set?"

I give Jess's and Harper's hands one last squeeze. "We are." I let them go ahead of me on the roped-off, grassy pathway to the stage.

Harper wears a flower-patterned sundress. Her curly hair is piled up on her head, the way it was for the March-break showcase. Jess is in her usual tank top and faded jeans. But her guitar hangs across her body on a brand-new, beautifully beaded strap that her mom, Louise, gave her this morning.

My mom surprised me this morning too. When Dad loaded Eric's hockey-camp gear into the car, Mom kissed them both goodbye, walked back up the driveway to where I was standing and wrapped her arm around me.

"You're not going?" I asked. I had resigned myself to the fact that my family simply didn't get my love for music.

"Hockey doesn't need me for once. Seeing you sing is all I want to do today."

She had planned it out with Louise the same day Jess came over to convince me to stay in Honeycomb.

Now Harper, Jess and I arrive backstage. I hear the chatter and laughter of the crowd. The volunteer gives a thumbs-up to Robert, who is waiting behind a large speaker on the stage. He looks suitably splendid with his dreadlocks and an embroidered tunic. He steps out and announces, "Music fans of all ages, you are in for a harmonious treat. Please give a warm, Tall Grass Young Performers welcome to...Honeycomb!"

* * *

Our first song starts smoothly. The tone is light and lilting. It seems to suit the mood of the audience. They're relaxed, happy to be here, heads bopping along, reminding me of Gabe's description of his first Tall Grass day.

I guess he's out there somewhere, but I don't have time to scan the crowd. I concentrate on Harper's voice, making sure my harmonies are solid and confident. She stands in the center, and Jess and I face each other, keeping eye contact so our timing is in sync.

Then we hit the chorus and Harper's voice hitches, like it's caught on something sharp. Her eyes widen for a split second, but she carries on.

In the next verse, Harper goes sharp on a high note. She backs slightly away from the mic, losing volume. I look her in the eye and start to sing the melody with her. She gives a tiny nod. Jess keeps her harmony going. We still sound okay, but my heart's whirling in my chest.

Harper keeps smiling, though, and that reminds me to make sure I am too. Grandma Barb told us smiling keeps our tone warm.

We make it to the last chorus, and I let Harper have the melody to herself again. She finishes strong.

Applause. My heart slows down, relieved to have gotten through the song. But I also feel like our time onstage is going by too quickly.

Jess and I take a step back. We've agreed that Harper should do the intro to the second song, as she did at the showcase.

Harper reaches down to get her water bottle, then smiles her best and brightest smile. "Thank you." Sunlight glints off her bracelets as she takes a quick drink. "My name's Harper Neale. How's everybody's day so far?"

The audience cheers. Looking out, I don't see Gabe, but I spot Darrell in the fourth row, his bald head sunburned, smiling proudly. A few rows back from him, Louise waves to Jess. Mom claps her hands above her head and woot-woots, a rowdy superfan.

"Yeah, it's feeling pretty great for us too," Harper continues. "We're gonna keep the day feeling great with this next song, 'Blue Skywriting.' Makes me think of the big blue sky we're all enjoying today." She lifts her hands, and the audience applauds some more.

Harper, the pro. I hope her parents are as proud of her as she is of them. They should be.

She looks at me and gives a tilt of her head. I come closer.

"This is Nat Boychuk," Harper says to the crowd. More clapping. "Nat's going to lead us in this beautiful song."

Lead? I swing my head to look at her and almost knock my chin on the mic. She puts her arm around me and whispers into my ear, "My voice won't do it justice. We all know you can do the melody."

Harper goes on. "Jess Lalonde there is going to work her guitar magic and sing her beautiful harmonies along with me."

As the audience claps, Harper switches places with me, so now I'm the one in front of the mic. She quietly says, "Show them how it's done."

I have a quick, vague sense of lots of happy faces looking up at me before I turn to Jess. Steady, calm Jess. My best friend. She counts us in.

Seventeen

We're at Jess's guitar solo before the song's bridge when I spot Gabe at the edge of the crowd. Our eyes connect. I remember how cold he was the last time we saw each other at Crescendo. I also remember how much he had wanted to be on this stage.

Holding his gaze, I sing, "*But the clouds, you brought them on / and the words you wrote, now they are gone / you've left me here, no sign of dawn.*"

Gabe mouths, "I'm sorry."

"*With your blue skywriting.*" Harper's and Jess's harmonies support me from either side. "*Bright blue skywriting.*" I turn to face the rest of the audience. The energy and happiness coming off the crowd make it feel like they're the fourth

141

member of Honeycomb. "*Blue skywriting swept me away*." Together, we bring the song home.

The applause sweeps onto the stage in a warm wave. I reach out my hands and Harper and Jess take them. We step away from the mic. I try to change places with Harper so she's in the middle again, but she shakes her head at me. "Stay right where you are," she whispers.

We bow. The clapping lasts a long time, long enough for me to know that I was right, back in March. That this—the music, the stage, the crowd—and all the hard work that led to this moment—is where I belong.

The first person to find us backstage is Gabe. "Honeycomb! You were awesome," he yells, giving Jess and Harper high fives.

He turns to me. As if by some secret code, Jess and Harper step away to take congratulations from other people.

"It's good to see you again," Gabe says.

"You too." He has more freckles than he did before. He looks sunnier.

"It was great to see you onstage. You got the melody back!"

I laugh. "Yeah, that was a bit of a surprise."

"Not to me." The hurt and angry Gabe is gone.

We move closer to each other. "I'm glad you came today," I say.

"Me too. Hey." Gabe puts his hand on my shoulder. "Did you notice who was standing beside me in the crowd?"

I shake my head.

"Middle-aged dude from Crescendo Music."

"Bushy-Beard!" I laugh.

"He's got a massive cheering voice. Pretty sure he's Honeycomb's biggest fan now. You better go visit him after all this."

"I will. If you come with me." I poke a finger lightly at his chest. "And if you promise you're going to try for Tall Grass again next year."

"Yeah, you better," Jess says. She and Harper are back beside us.

"I will," Gabe says. "In fact, I already know one of the songs I'm going to work on. But I might need your help."

Harper, sucking on one of her throat lozenges, says, "You do know Nat's a singer, not a banjo player?"

Gabe hasn't taken his eyes off me. "There's whistling in this song. I happen to know she's quite the whistler."

"I'd love to help you," I say.

Then we're surrounded by Louise and Mom and Darrell. Hugs, handshakes, more hugs. Grandma Barb arrives with Harper's parents, who give off so much music-biz shine it's easy to see where Harper gets her confidence.

"After-party at my house," Grandma Barb announces. "I insist!"

We move like a friendly swarm away from the stage. Darrell and Gabe talk about acts they saw earlier. Louise and Mom chat with Grandma Barb. I hear "I'm embarrassed to say I had no idea they were that good" from Mom, and "Oh, yes" from Grandma Barb. Just ahead of me, Harper links arms with her mom and dad.

"Now that's an impressive trio." I point as Jess comes over to me.

"Imagine the egos if they rehearsed together."

"Hey, Harper gave me the melody today." I bump against Jess. "I've got to thank her for that."

"True." Jess bumps back. "It's important for the lead singer to thank her backup singers."

That stops me short. "You guys are not my backup singers! We're equal. A trio."

"I was teasing." Jess laughs, hitching her guitar case over her shoulder. "I know we're equal. I think Harper finally realizes we are too. Thanks to you."

I smile at my best friend. "We're Honeycomb."

Jess slings her arm around me. "We are."

Acknowledgments

Thank you to Bronwyn, Caroline and David for your love and support throughout the *Honeycomb*-building process. To my brilliant writing-group pals, Pat Bourke, Karen Krossing, Karen Rankin and Erin Thomas, thanks for being my first readers. Writing takes brains and heart, and you are generous in sharing yours with me. I sing the praises of Sarah Harvey, who created the Limelights series, and Robin Stevenson, my editor, for their professionalism and enthusiasm. To everyone at Orca Book Publishers, a round of applause for working so hard to bring quality books to young readers. Finally, thank you to the countless musicians who provided the inspiration for (and soundtrack to) writing this book. As Harper says, "Music knows everything."

PATRICIA McCOWAN originally wanted to be an actor. She took acting classes as a kid, was a drama club nerd in high school and studied acting at the University of Winnipeg and the Banff Centre. After acting for a while (and then becoming a mom), she directed her creative energies to writing. Her short stories have appeared in YA anthologies, as well as in print and online magazines. *Honeycomb* is her first novel. Visit patriciamccowan.com for more information.